D1626992

BABY DREAMS IN GOOD HOPE

CINDY KIRK

WAVERLY
HOUSE

Marigold Rallis pushed aside the sadness, determined to enjoy Sunday dinner with her family. Though she considered herself an optimist, she'd learned over the past two years that infertility pressure could bring down even the staunchest glass-half-full gal.

Everyone around the elegant table was in high spirits, filled with anticipation of the upcoming wedding of Marigold's stepsister.

The solid presence of her husband, Cade, beside her was a steadying force. Her mood lifted when he clasped her hand and brought it to his lips. Cade was the one bright light in the battle they waged together.

"You look especially lovely this evening," he murmured.

She smiled, knowing the recently added copper highlights gave dimension to her natural honey-blond color.

Across the table, two of Marigold's sisters spoke in hushed tones.

"Word is... You have to..." was all she heard.

Then Fin spoke tersely, her voice taut with a steely edge. "I have to tell Marigold and Prim first."

Marigold took a bite of dessert and wondered what Fin needed to tell her and Prim. She tried to tune her ears to hear more, but the tinkling sound of a spoon against crystal interrupted the conversation.

"May I please have everyone's attention?" Lynn's blue eyes seemed to project extra warmth when her gaze briefly landed on Marigold.

Seeing the love in her dad's eyes when he shifted toward his new wife had Marigold's heart swelling. She rested her head against the side of her husband's shoulder.

Lynn cleared her throat. "I've heard rumors we're going to have another baby in the family by the end of the year. Anyone care to share their news now so I don't have to learn about it in the Open Door?"

Laughter rippled around the table.

Marigold sat upright as all eyes shifted toward her and Cade. Everyone knew they'd been trying for years to have a baby. Now they all thought that happy dream had been realized.

Cade's hand gripped hers under the table.

Marigold saw Ami glance at Fin. Something about the look, along with the snippet of conversation she'd overheard between the two, had the pressure in her chest turning painful.

"I don't know why you're all looking at me." Marigold cursed the tremble in her voice. "If Cade and I had that kind of news to share, we'd be shouting it from the top of Eagle Tower. Heck, we'd probably spring for a full-page ad in the Open Door."

Cade slipped an arm around her shoulders.

"When that happens, and *it will happen*," Cade's steady gaze met Marigold's before he shifted his focus to Lynn, "you won't have to ask."

Two bright splotches of pink cut a swath across Lynn's ivory cheeks. "I'm sorry. I must have—"

"It's not Marigold who's pregnant. It's me." Fin shot her youngest sister an apologetic glance.

Everything in Marigold went cold.

Not fair. The words circled in her head so fiercely that for a second Marigold feared she might blurt them out.

Fin's gaze was gentle on Marigold's face. "Jeremy and I were waiting until—"

"You?" Marigold choked out the word. "You just had a baby. Eddie is barely three months old. How can you be pregnant again?"

"I wanted to tell you and the rest of the family privately before news got out. I should have acted sooner." Fin glanced at Ami. "Ami heard the same rumor as Lynn. The Good Hope gossip mill must have somehow gotten wind that one of the Bloom sisters purchased a pregnancy test last week at the General Store."

"Last week?" Marigold's voice rose as she shook off Cade's staying hand. "You've known since last week?"

"Cut her some slack, Marigold." Jeremy's tone held a warning.

"The idea of having two babies so close together came as quite a shock. But we're very excited." Fin's gaze swept to the bassinette where Eddie slept. Her lips curved in a soft, maternal smile.

"We're thrilled." Jeremy spoke firmly once again when Marigold opened her mouth. "We hope you share our joy."

Marigold wanted to share their joy. Fin was her sister and she loved her. But Fin already had a baby, while she had none.

Though she tried desperately to paste on a smile, Marigold couldn't make her lips cooperate. Worse, she felt a tear slide down her cheek.

Compassion filled Fin's eyes, and she opened her mouth.

Marigold shook her head vigorously. One word of sympathy, and she would dissolve in a puddle of tears.

"Congratulations, Fin and Jeremy." Her father broke the uncomfortable silence by lifting his wineglass. "A toast. To new beginnings."

Everyone lifted their glasses, and well-wishes soon flowed as generously as the wine. After a moment, Marigold managed to pull it together enough to add her congratulations.

Once the dinner ended, Cade stayed close, a hand resting on her shoulder or an arm around her waist, a supportive presence at her side. Then a call from one of his deputies had him stepping away for a few minutes.

When talk in the living room turned from last-minute wedding details to babies, Marigold excused herself and opened the door to the terrace.

She realized immediately she wasn't alone. Her breath came out in a relieved whoosh when she realized it was her dad. Steve Bloom sat in a white lacquered rocking chair, his gaze focused on the brilliance of the setting sun.

He turned, smiled and motioned her over. "Join me."

Marigold's heart stuttered. Her father had always been her rock. She knew without a doubt she could lean on him. She dropped down to sit beside him.

Concern filled his hazel eyes. "How are you holding up?"

"The news…well, it took me by surprise." Marigold swallowed hard. "But I'm happy for Jeremy and Fin."

He reached over and squeezed her hand. "We're all happy for them."

Maybe she was reading too much into his steady gaze, maybe she was seeing what she wanted to see, but Marigold thought he wished she were the pregnant one, too.

"Lynn feels horrible," he began. "She—"

"I can see why she thought it was me." Her bottom lip began to tremble as longing rose inside her. "When is it going to be my turn, Daddy? I'm starting to think it'll never happen."

He rose and pulled her to standing with him. Then he wrapped his arms around her and held her close, stroking her hair the way he used to when she'd been a child wanting her mother.

Just as she had all those years ago, in her father's arms, she found solace.

CHAPTER ONE

"Cade is not cheating on you." Amaryllis Cross looked up from the mixer, a splotch of powdered sugar on her cheek.

"Ami's right." Marigold's other sister, Primrose, echoed the sentiment from her position at the table. Even as she spoke, Prim took the cooled "puppy chow" from the baking sheet and put it into a resealable plastic bag. "Your husband adores you. He would never cheat."

The four Bloom sisters had gathered in the huge kitchen at Rakes Farm on Tuesday afternoon in preparation for tomorrow's Wacky Wednesday celebration. Except this one would be extra special. The Bloom sisters planned to surprise their stepmother, Lynn Chapin, with a party.

Lynn had celebrated her sixtieth birthday last week at the home she shared with her husband, Steve. It had been an elegant affair, much like the woman herself, beginning with champagne and appetizers and ending with her favorite dessert, bananas Foster.

This celebration, complete with cake, Neapolitan ice cream squares and fruit punch, would be a chance for the grandkids to show their love for their grandmother. With everyone busy with activities, holding the party on an already-scheduled Wacky Wednesday made sense.

The weekly Wednesday get-togethers of the blended Bloom and Chapin families had begun as a way to allow the cousins to have fun together and so the adults could hang out, too.

The wonderful woman her father married would never see this coming. Marigold was doing her best to embrace the party spirit. Normally, she looked forward to events like these, especially when the party involved surprising someone she loved.

Instead of the joy she'd have felt even six months ago, a rise of mixed emotions swamped the youngest Bloom sister.

Love and marriage—her own—had been in her thoughts often these past few weeks. She loved her husband, Sheriff Cade Rallis, with her entire heart. Cade was everything to her. She'd once thought her marriage invincible, but lately she'd begun to worry about cracks.

"Earth to Marigold." Delphinium's voice broke through her reverie.

Marigold's head jerked up, and she found herself gazing into Fin's piercing emerald-green eyes.

"I won't tell you Cade wouldn't cheat, because Prim is right. The guy adores you." Fin waved a hand in the air. "You need to tell us why you fear he might."

That was Fin, Marigold thought, going straight to the heart of the matter.

After placing another sugared lemon slice atop the pink lemonade cake she'd baked, Marigold expelled a shaky breath. She'd tried not to think about the phone call, but it was always in her thoughts. She didn't even have to close her eyes to recall his hushed tone. The urgency in his voice and the emotion.

Lost in that horrible memory, Marigold didn't even slap Ami's hand away when her sister dipped a finger in the bowl of leftover lemon-butter frosting.

"I heard him speaking with his ex-fiancée on the phone."

Marigold's heart squeezed, and tears flooded her eyes. It felt as if she'd done more crying over the past few weeks than she'd done in all her years on this earth. "Low and quiet. He thought I was upstairs."

"How did he get her number?" Ami asked. "Or, rather, how did she get his?"

"I don't know." Marigold shook her head, misery heavy around her shoulders.

"You ran into her a couple of months ago." Prim's brows pulled together. Unlike Marigold's honey-blond hair, Prim's hair and brows had a distinct hint of red.

"I remember now. In Milwaukee." Ami rested her back against the counter. "You and Cade went to a Brewers game at Miller Park."

"I thought Alice was still in Detroit. I'd never met her before." Marigold paused to get her rioting emotions under control. "She was—*is* incredibly lovely. She was very friendly. To both of us."

"Not married?" Prim added.

"No. Not married. She was there with a girlfriend. Alice told us she'd recently relocated to Milwaukee for her job." Marigold shrugged. "That was the extent of the conversation."

She hadn't thought much about Alice since that day. Cade certainly hadn't mentioned her. Yet, the woman had his private cell number. There was no way she could have gotten it…without him giving it to her.

It was a realization Marigold hadn't wanted to face. Cade was her soul mate, and the thought of his possible duplicity cut to the core.

"What did Cade say when you asked him why he was talking with her on the phone?" With great skill, Fin circled the conversation back to her original question. Though her voice remained easy, the baby strapped to her chest stirred as if sensing the tension in the air.

When Marigold hesitated, Fin's gaze bore into her, like a heat-seeking missile finding its target. "You *did* ask him to explain."

A low tolerance for bullshit was something she and Fin shared.

Marigold lifted her chin. "Yes. I asked him."

"Good. I'm proud of you." Fin picked up a piece of wrapped chocolate from the large work counter and tossed it to her youngest sister. "What did he say?"

"He was evasive." Tears once again filled Marigold's eyes as she looked down at the candy in her hand. She hated, hated, hated the tears that came so easily now. Even as a small child, Marigold had never been the poor-me sort.

In the early years of their infertility struggles, she and Cade had been so hopeful. They were young and healthy and willing to do whatever was necessary to achieve a pregnancy.

The determination was still there, but that once-bright light of hope had been reduced to smoldering embers. Marigold knew Cade desperately wanted to be a father, and she felt as if she'd failed him.

The knowledge that the fertility issues were on her end—not his—added its own stress. Despite the hope and prayers, it was beginning to look as if their struggles would never bear fruit.

"Examples." Fin's brusque tone belied the sympathy in her eyes. "Tell us exactly who said what, little sister. We need all the information in order to help you sort this out."

This time, when tears slipped down Marigold's cheeks, she was powerless to stop them. Ami switched off the mixer and moved to sit beside her sister, wrapping an arm around her shoulders while casting a pointed glance at Fin.

"Hey. I'm not the bad guy here." Fin lifted her shoulders, causing the baby to fuss. A couple of gentle strokes on the back of her son's silky blond curls had him settling. "Just trying to dig up the facts."

"I know you mean well." Marigold cast Fin a watery smile. "I'm sorry I'm so scattered. I've just been so tired lately."

Concern blanketed Ami's face. "You're not sleeping?"

"I sleep all the time." Marigold offered a chuckle. "I feel like all I do is sleep. I think all the stress of the past year has finally caught up with me."

"After Rory died," Prim said, referring to her first husband, "all I wanted to do was sleep."

"No one died, and I'm still a mess." Marigold lifted her hands, let them drop. "It's no wonder Cade wants Alice."

"Hey, you're not a mess. You're a strong, independent woman who handles whatever is tossed your way." Fin's expression turned fierce. "You'll confront this latest challenge in the same way."

"Fin is right." Prim handed Marigold a napkin, her voice as soft as melted butter. "To help, we need the facts."

"Take a couple of deep breaths," Ami told her.

After doing as her sister instructed, Marigold felt herself steady. She took one more breath for good measure, then focused on the cake. It was hard enough to share without seeing the sympathy in her sisters' eyes. "Like I said, he thought I'd gone upstairs, but I was still in the kitchen. I heard him say her name and—"

"How did he say her name? With feeling? Or did he just say it more matter-of-factly?" Ami asked.

Marigold thought back to the call that had solidified all her fears. "There was warmth in his voice and a lot of emotion."

Ami expelled a breath and glanced at her other sisters, who'd taken seats at the table.

It reminded Marigold of their younger selves, before her sisters had married and had children. Back when they'd sit around a table drinking wine and eating chocolate and talking out their problems.

Now she and Cade were the only ones without kids. From the

start, they'd both wanted children more than anything. Had they been so focused on the idea of becoming parents that somewhere along the way they'd forgotten to also be a couple?

Marigold realized that as much as she wanted a baby, she wanted her husband more. She could live without children. She couldn't imagine life without Cade.

More tears fell.

"Marigold." Fin's tone held a warning and a gentle nudge.

"He was talking really low, and I could only catch a couple of words. 'Milwaukee' and 'yes, I definitely want to explore.'"

"Explore what?" Prim's brows drew together.

"I don't know." Marigold sniffled, wiped her nose with the napkin in her hand. "Maybe a relationship."

"Did he say that?" Fin demanded.

"No."

"Then don't go there," Fin ordered.

Ami squeezed her hand. "Remember, innocent until proven guilty."

Marigold drew a shuddering breath and nodded.

Fin made a circular motion with one hand. "Tell us what you heard."

"Just the facts, ma'am." Prim spoke in a voice designed to lighten the mood.

Marigold shot her sister a smile. A smile that quickly faded.

"Like I said, all I heard him say was 'Milwaukee' and 'I definitely want to explore.' I walked into the room while he was still on the phone with her." Marigold straightened in the chair. "He got off quickly. I asked him who he was speaking with."

It seemed as if her sisters held their collective breaths, much as she had that afternoon.

"He said it was Alice, his former friend from Detroit."

Fin shook her head. "He didn't lie, no, but Alice isn't just a 'former friend.' She's his former fiancée."

Prim gave Fin a stern look as she unwrapped a piece of

chocolate. "Come on. They were engaged briefly, and it was ages ago. Long before he even met Marigold."

Prim passed the chocolate to Marigold, who promptly popped it into her mouth. She took a deep breath and continued. "He reminded me that she recently moved to Milwaukee for her job. She wanted to discuss some Wisconsin laws. He answered her questions."

"Did you ask how she got his cell number?" Fin asked.

"I did. His answers all made sense. He ran into her at a seminar he was attending in Milwaukee. That's when he gave her his number. He told me she'd like it if we could all get together sometime."

"How long ago was this phone call?" Prim asked.

"Two weeks," Marigold told Prim.

"Why are we only hearing about this now?" Fin asked.

"I told myself my fears were silly. Cade is so kind and loving, and he's an honorable man. Cheating is not in his DNA. I almost convinced myself I was being silly when—"

Around the small table, the sisters all leaned forward.

"I saw a text." Conscious of Fin's desire for all the facts, Marigold continued. "It was from Alice asking if he could meet her in Milwaukee today. That was last week."

"Did you ask him about it?"

Marigold shook her head. "I didn't want him to know I snooped."

"He's working today, right?" Ami's brows drew together in thought. "He works on Tuesdays."

"He left the house at his usual time." Marigold clasped her hands together to still their trembling. "I called the station, and they said he took the morning off. Something to do with business he needed to take care of in Milwaukee."

"Well…" Fin blew out a breath. "That isn't good."

"Cade wouldn't cheat on you." Ami placed a hand on Marigold's arm. "I've seen how he looks at you. He loves you,

Marigold."

"There has to be an explanation," Prim insisted. "We just have to figure out what it is."

~

Over dinner that night, Marigold studied her husband. Cade had come home at a normal time and appeared in high spirits. Though she'd given him plenty of opportunity, he hadn't mentioned a trip to Milwaukee.

"This pot roast is amazing." He smiled at her from across the table, a handsome man with brown hair and broad shoulders. It was the twinkle in those dark eyes that had first captured her attention.

Cade was fun and sweet, and by God, he was hers. Alice had had her chance. She wouldn't get a second one, not if Marigold had anything to say about it.

"This wine goes perfectly with the meat." He glanced at her glass as if noticing for the first time that hers held water. "You're not having any?"

She shook her head. "My stomach has been upset, and it didn't taste right. Probably all those cookies I chowed down on at Fin's today."

"That's right, you were doing party planning on your day off." Admiration filled his eyes. "It amazes me how much you get done. One of these days, you'll need to hire someone at the salon to take off some of the load."

"Actually, I've been emailing back and forth with Charlotte McCray. Do you remember her?"

He cocked his head. "She owns Golden Door."

"Her salon was my main competitor when I moved here." Marigold's and Golden Door weren't the only hair salons in town, but both were considered a cut above the others in quality of services. "Once Charlotte left Good Hope, the woman who took over for her, well, she wasn't a particularly skilled stylist. Or as good of a businesswoman."

"Is Charlotte thinking of coming back?"

"Actually, she is, which is surprising considering how eager she was to leave." Marigold's lips curved. "We're discussing the possibility of going into business together."

Cade lifted the wineglass to his lips. "Really?"

"My client load is out of control. When you add in the customers who come in from other states for my services and expect me to fit them in, well, you know what it's been like for me."

"You make carrying a heavy load appear effortless." He reached across the table, and the simple touch of his warm hand had her heart weeping. "I can't believe how you've continued to build your business, despite all the infertility stuff the past couple of years."

"If things work out, and we have a child—"

"There's no 'if' about it." His fingers tightened around hers. "We *will* have a child. Whether it's the usual way or as a result of adoption."

The fierce certainty in his voice steadied her and gave her strength. How many times along this journey had she been tempted to give up?

"I'm terrified we're going to get picked by a birth mother who changes her mind at the last minute."

"What's meant to be will be." Cade studied her for a long moment. "Now, tell me how you're considering working Charlotte into your business plan."

See? It isn't that difficult to have a conversation, Marigold thought twenty minutes later as they sat on the sofa, his arm looped around her shoulders.

When he began to nuzzle her neck, Marigold cleared her throat. "I called the station today."

He lifted his head, surprise on his face. "Why didn't you just call my cell?"

Because, she wanted to tell him, there had been times recently when she'd had difficulty reaching him on it. She simply shrugged. "I don't know. I was surprised when they told me you took the morning off."

The guarded expression that filled his eyes had her heart sinking. Still, she pressed forward. "I understand you went to Milwaukee." When he said nothing, Marigold felt compelled to fill the silence. "I'm surprised you didn't mention it."

"Not much to say." He smiled, took her hand and brought her ice-cold fingers to his lips for a kiss. "Quick business trip."

"What kind of business?"

His dark eyes narrowed. "Why all the questions?"

"Why all the hesitation in answering?" Marigold managed—barely—to keep her tone light. "Unless you have something to hide. Do you have something to hide, Cade?"

The guilt in his eyes was unmistakable, and her heart lurched. She blinked back tears. She would not cry. She would take this time and find out what was really going on between him and Alice. Then she would deal with it.

"Marigold." He met her gaze. "I've—"

His phone squawked, a ringtone she recognized as coming from the sheriff's office. He yanked it from his pocket. "I need to take this."

"Rallis," he said into his phone, then listened. "I'll be right there."

"Cade." Standing now, as was he, she grabbed his arm. "Don't go."

"I have to," he told her with what appeared to be sincere regret. "There's been a bad accident out on the highway. My deputies need extra support."

She couldn't hold him back from his duty, couldn't insist that he sit down and finish their personal conversation before heading out to help.

Instead, Marigold forced her lips into a semblance of a smile. "Be safe."

He bent over and brushed her lips with his. "Back soon."

She stood at the window and watched him leave. Only then did she let the tears fall.

CHAPTER TWO

Marigold let her gaze wander over the scene for this week's Wacky Wednesday dinner. The large expanse of lawn behind the house at Rakes Farm was a beautiful setting for the get-together. In addition to family, several close friends had been invited. Ruby Rakes, Fin's grandmother-in-law, was there, along with a couple of her best buddies.

Standing by herself beneath a leafy oak tree, Marigold felt a sense of trepidation when she caught Ruby's closest friend, Gladys Bertholf, staring. Gladys, the ninetysomething matriarch of Good Hope, had many talents. One of them was her Madame Gitana persona. During various events held in the town square, Gladys would set up a tent, bring her crystal and tell fortunes.

Her sisters, especially Ami, had encouraged Marigold to have her do a reading, ask Gladys what she saw in her crystal regarding a baby for her and Cade. Marigold had resisted the urge to see too far into her future.

She wasn't sure she wanted to know if her and Cade's quest to have a child, whether through conceiving or adoption, would be successful.

Ami was convinced Gladys was legit. Even more reason,

Marigold thought, to keep her distance. Especially now that she was worried about her relationship with Cade.

She could survive not having children, but she wasn't certain she could survive losing Cade. Especially to a former girlfriend who could likely give him the children he so desperately wanted. Children that, as of now, she couldn't.

Keeping her distance from Gladys proved surprisingly easy. In addition to Marigold, her three sisters and their families, her stepmother's three children and their families were out in force.

She smiled, her gaze lingering on Cade as he played badminton with several of the older children.

"He'll make an excellent father."

Marigold had been so focused on her handsome husband she hadn't seen, or even felt, Prim move to stand beside her. Two of Prim's kids—twin sons Connor and Callum—were playing the game, as well as Prim's husband, Max.

Marigold had spotted Prim's youngest child, Adelyn, a few minutes ago, one arm hooked around her grandfather's neck.

Prim leaned close and pointed, a wide smile on her lips. "Look at the way Cade's teasing Callum. The boys adore him."

"If he sticks with me, I don't know that he'll get a chance to be a father."

The elbow to the ribs would have been expected from Fin, or even Ami, but not from sweet and mild-mannered Prim. Then again, Prim was made of strong stuff. Hadn't she raised rambunctious twin boys on her own for several years after their father died, back before she and Max got together?

"Hey." Marigold glared at Prim. "What was that for?"

"For being a stupid-ass."

Marigold widened her eyes. "Since when do you talk like that, Primrose Bloom?"

Prim waved an airy hand. "I learned it from the boys."

"Since when do you and Max let them talk that way?"

"We don't." Prim grinned. "They know better now."

"I'm not being stupid, just realistic." Marigold held up her hands and took a step back when Prim's eyes shot blue fire.

"No," Prim told her, "you're being a stupid-ass. I thought you and Cade decided that after you tried the fertility stuff you'd go for adoption. If that didn't work, you'd foster."

"We did decide that." Marigold heaved a breath.

"Where are you with the adoption process?" Prim demanded.

"Everything is done. We even passed the home visit." Marigold gave a little hiccup of a laugh, recalling the celebration. "We were both so excited, we went out for dinner at Sombreros and celebrated."

"Best Mexican food on the peninsula and really amazing margaritas." Prim's eyes grew soft. "What happens now?"

"We wait. We hope that a couple will pick us." The smile that had lifted Marigold's lips at the memory of those amazing margaritas faded. "The social worker warned it can sometimes take years."

"It won't. Not for you and Cade."

"You don't know that."

"Sometimes you just have to believe."

"My belief in a lot of things is being sorely tested these days." Marigold's gaze shifted to Cade.

"What about private adoption? David went that route. He said it didn't take long for him and Whitney to get Brynn."

David Chapin—Lynn's eldest—and his first wife had adopted Brynn as an infant through a private adoption brokered by an attorney in Chicago.

"We've discussed that option. Since we sold the land, we have the money. But..." Marigold hesitated.

"Marigold, honey." Prim's touch was like a soothing balm on her frayed emotions. "You can tell me anything. You know that, right?"

"This whole trying-to-have-a-baby thing has been hard on

me." Marigold blew out a breath. "You know me, Prim. I'm as strong as they come."

"The strongest," Prim agreed.

"I told Cade I don't know if I can stand having a birth mother change her mind at the last minute. I don't think it's uncommon, and while I understand they need to be sure, I…"

Her sister offered an encouraging smile, even as her eyes remained somber.

"I feel off my game," Marigold said. "Not strong." When those blasted tears once again formed in her eyes, she swiped them away. She would not ruin Lynn's party by bawling like a baby. "I don't know what's wrong with me."

"Sweetie, you've been through so much." Prim wrapped her arms around her, her voice as soothing as a mother's caress. "Have you considered talking to Liam or Trinity?"

Liam Gallagher and Trinity Goodhue owned Connections, a local counseling center. Marigold knew several people who'd gone there and been helped.

"If I continue to feel like this, I might." Dry-eyed now, Marigold gazed over the yard, the sounds of laughter and conversation sliding off of her. "I've been done with the fertility drugs for nearly three months. I should be feeling better, shouldn't I?"

Concern filled Prim's eyes. "Are your hormones still out of whack?"

Marigold gave a little laugh. "If by out of whack, you mean no period, PMS symptoms and sore breasts, then yes."

Prim stilled, and a look Marigold couldn't decipher filled her eyes. "You haven't had a period since you went off the drugs?"

"The doctor warned me it might take a while for my system to get back to normal." Marigold attempted a nonchalant shrug. "She said it happens a lot after you go off fertility drugs."

"Do you…" Prim paused to clear her throat, appeared to be

carefully considering her next words. "Do you think you could be...pregnant?"

Marigold was embarrassed to admit her heart gave a sudden leap. Even after so many negative pregnancy tests, the response told her she hadn't given up hope. Still, wanting something, hoping desperately for something, didn't mean she was going to be, well, a stupid-ass about it.

"I suppose anything is possible." Marigold couldn't quite keep the hitch from her voice as she added, "Though it's not likely."

"What's not likely?" Fin sauntered up with four-month-old Eddie in her arms. The tiny White Sox ball cap that covered his blond curls coordinated with his baseball onesie.

Unlike most babies, Eddie had retained the head of lustrous hair he'd been born with. Marigold had once envisioned the same hair on her own child when she'd dreamed what her and Cade's baby might look like.

"I repeat," Fin spoke with a little more force, "what's not likely?"

The thought of never cradling a child in her arms like Fin was doing now had Marigold bristling. "Did you ever think that maybe we're having a private conversation and that what we're discussing is none of your business?"

Fin's green eyes narrowed, then she grinned. "Whatever goes on between my baby sisters is my business."

Marigold couldn't help but laugh. She shot Prim a warning glance. She understood Prim speculating, but she didn't want the rumor starting up again that she might be pregnant.

Several weeks earlier, when rumors had spread that one of the Bloom sisters was pregnant, everyone assumed it was her. It hadn't been her. It was Fin, pregnant again after having her first child only months earlier. No, Marigold definitely didn't want the speculation to start up again.

"It's not likely Connor and Callum will beat Max and Cade."

Marigold gestured with one hand to where the badminton game raged.

"Someone needs to tell the twins." Prim's smile widened. "They're definitely going for gold."

"Your boys are growing into fine young men, Primrose."

Marigold stiffened at the sound of Gladys's voice. She hadn't seen the woman approach. Hadn't realized the older woman, who saw too much, stood right beside her until it was too late to make an exit.

"Thank you, Gladys." Prim smiled. "Max and I are very proud of them."

"They adore Eddie." Fin rubbed her son's back. "They're so gentle with him."

Marigold felt the pressure build as she realized it was her turn to add to the discussion.

Keep it general, Marigold told herself. One thing was for certain: She'd definitely do her part to keep the discussion off of her and Cade.

Thankfully, Gladys loved to talk, and she ended the momentary silence. "This is a lovely birthday celebration." Her gaze shifted momentarily across the yard to Lynn and the sisters' father. "They're an amazing couple."

That, Marigold thought, was a statement everyone could get behind. She smiled as her father gave his wife a one-armed hug. Left alone to raise four girls after his wife died, Steve Bloom had shouldered the heavy load with strength, grace and a healthy dose of good humor. He'd dated other women, but he'd told his daughters that Lynn was the one he'd waited for all these years.

Lynn had waited, too. She and her husband had been Good Hope's power couple. They owned and ran a network of banks and had their fingers in a variety of commercial real estate ventures. They were known for holding the most elegant parties.

Then, under immense stress during the 2008 banking crisis, Robert had collapsed after a sudden heart attack and died. Lynn, strong as they came, soldiered on and brought all their business enterprises back from the brink of collapse.

Unlike Marigold's father, Lynn had rarely dated during the years following her spouse's death. She'd preferred to focus on business. No one had seen a marriage between the business tycoon and the high school teacher coming.

Fin smiled at Gladys. "The dinner at their home on Sunday was lovely, but we wanted to do something fun where all the grandchildren could be involved. Also, we wanted to open up the celebration to more of her friends and ours."

"It's been a few years since I've been a child, but I enjoyed today's menu immensely." Gladys chuckled. "I had two hot dog sliders. The mango-pineapple salsa topping was inspired."

Though Marigold had vowed to keep her eyes on the badminton game and off of Gladys, she found herself shifting to face the woman.

Tonight's menu had been developed with children in mind. In addition to the sliders, there was pizza monkey bread and baked mac and cheese. The only relatively normal addition to the menu was the pink lemonade birthday cake Marigold had baked.

"Lynn must be proud when she looks out on such a lovely family. You've all done a fine job of merging the two." Gladys expelled a satisfied breath.

The merging had taken some effort, but hadn't been difficult, as most of the adult children of both Steve and Lynn were already friends. Marigold refocused on the badminton game. Brynn had entered the game and was proving to be a fierce competitor. She was showing the boys and the two men just how the game should be played.

Marigold's heart gave a ping. Yes, even the grandchildren were forging a closeness.

"Ruby is thrilled you'll be giving her another great-grandchild early next year."

Gladys's words were like a knife to Marigold's heart. Selfishly, all she could think was it should have been her. Fin had a baby, right there in her arms, while Marigold's arms remained empty.

"Jeremy and I are super excited." Fin gave a little laugh. "Though we're definitely going to be busy."

"Hoping for another boy?" Gladys arched a brow. "Or a little girl this time?"

"A healthy baby." Fin nodded for emphasis. "That's all we want."

Marigold knew her sister meant every word. Years after the fact, the family had learned Fin had suffered a miscarriage in high school. Her sister had borne that pain all alone, not even telling Jeremy until years later.

That was one thing about her and Cade, Marigold thought. They'd been together in this battle to have a baby from the beginning. He'd gone with her to her doctors' appointments and experienced the heartbreak with her when the pregnancy tests turned up negative time after time.

When Gladys turned that assessing gaze to her, Marigold braced herself. "I understand you and Cade will close on the Dunlevey house on the fifteenth."

Marigold exhaled the breath she hadn't realized she was holding. Talking about houses was something she could handle. "We can't wait. The house is amazing. It will make a wonderful home."

"Plus, you'll be just down the road from Ami and Beck," Fin pointed out.

Marigold laughed. "A cross I'll have to bear."

The truth was, both she and Cade were excited to live so near to Ami and her husband. Though selling the property they'd owned that faced Green Bay had been a difficult decision, she and Cade really didn't have the money to build.

Now, they owned a beautiful historic home close to her salon and the sheriff's office. A large home they hoped to one day fill with children.

That was the plan. Marigold's gaze shifted to Cade.

As if her husband felt her eyes on him, he turned and grinned, offering a wave and a wink before refocusing on the game.

A rush of love enveloped Marigold.

"He's a handsome devil, your husband," Gladys said to Marigold.

"That he is."

"He'll make a wonderful father," Gladys added.

"Yes." Clearing her throat, Marigold smiled brightly in the direction where Steve Bloom was bent over, setting up the croquet course. "My father appears to need my assistance. I'll be—"

Before Marigold could beat a hasty retreat, Gladys's bony fingers curved around her arm in a tight grasp. "Change is coming. Big changes. Be ready."

Big changes. What did Gladys mean?

Only a few times in Marigold's life had she found herself unable to catch her breath. The first had been when she'd been ten. She'd lost control of her bike and slammed into a telephone pole. The force of the impact had knocked the air from her lungs.

The second had been when her mother was diagnosed with leukemia. Marigold had been in middle school. When her parents had broken the news to their daughters, Marigold had cried until she couldn't breathe.

And now.

Somehow, Marigold managed a jerky nod and hurried off. She wanted to run, to sprint across the yard to her dad. To have him wrap his arms around her and reassure her that everything was going to be okay. Tell her that her husband loved her more than life itself.

But she was twenty-eight, not eight, and he was busy setting up the croquet game. Ami's Sarah Rose and Prim's Adelyn hovered close, "helping." When Marigold was far enough away that she didn't think Gladys would follow, she veered off and headed down to the water.

Rakes Pond was where groups played pond hockey and where children of all ages skated whenever ice covered the water. It was deserted now, and when she sank onto one of the benches along the perimeter, Marigold finally found her breath.

"Is everything okay?"

Bea Appleton, one of Marigold's friends, stood a distance away. The sparkling diamond on her left hand caught the rays of the sun and sent them scattering in a rainbow of color. Several weeks earlier, Bea had become engaged to Lynn's son Clay.

Marigold had been excited that her friend, the sweet and gentle Bea, would now be a part of the family. Never one for high fashion, the bookseller sported one of her favorite graphic tees. This one showed a stack of books and announced, "Books… Because Reality Is Overrated."

"Everything is fine," Marigold told her friend. "I just need some alone time."

Bea's eyes, appearing almost violet in the light, were solemn. "I came down here for the same reason."

Marigold appreciated that Bea didn't ask a lot of questions or push for answers. She simply made it clear she was available should Marigold need her.

"I won't be long," Marigold assured her.

What was wrong with her? Marigold wondered as she watched her friend trudge up the hill. Those fertility drugs really had done a number on her system. And her psyche.

Sitting alone when there was a party going on? Crying at the drop of a hat?

Not to mention being so exhausted she could barely make it through a day without a nap. She was aware such fatigue could be a sign of depression. Yet, she didn't feel particularly depressed.

And then all the PMS symptoms that simply wouldn't go away. Last night, she'd snapped at Cade when he'd asked a simple question, then cried when she saw the confused look on his face.

Marigold would consult with her doctor, that's what she

would do. She would make an appointment tomorrow and get something to start her period. Once her cycle was regular, hopefully she'd start feeling like herself again.

Maybe her worry over Cade was justified, but one conversation did not an affair make. The trip to Milwaukee? Well, there was a logical explanation. Once they had a chance to sit down and talk, he'd tell her all about it. She might even confide her fears.

Marigold trusted her husband. She loved her husband.

Once she got her hormones under control, things would be better.

CHAPTER THREE

On the way home from the party, Cade detoured to the Dunlevey mansion. Though that's what everyone in Good Hope called the old Victorian, it wasn't really a mansion, simply a large brick home built in the late 1880s. It was only one of a handful of homes in the county to survive from that era.

"I can't believe it's ours." Marigold stood with Cade in the driveway of the now-empty house.

"It does seem surreal." Cade chuckled. "I never thought I'd own a home with a cupola."

He'd positioned himself at Marigold's side once they got out of the truck, and his arm was slung around her shoulders.

Marigold knew he loved this house, but couldn't help wondering if he harbored regrets over selling the land they'd both loved. "I know you really wanted to build a home facing the bay."

"I want a home with you now. Not in five years." He surprised —and pleased—her by bending down and kissing her gently on the mouth. His arm tightened around her shoulders. "That's how long it'd have been before we could afford a house that would do justice to that lot. This way, we have a beautiful home just down the street from your sister."

"No regrets?" She searched his eyes and realized she wasn't just talking about the lot, but their life together.

"Not a one." His gaze lingered on her face, and she saw the puzzlement there. "You've seemed different lately. Everything okay?"

He'd asked her basically the same question in a dozen different ways over the past few weeks. Each time, she'd assured him that nothing was wrong. Each time, he'd pretended to believe her.

"I've been feeling really strange lately. Dr. Swanson warned me that might happen, coming off the drugs, but I find myself wanting to sleep all day. And I cry all the damn time."

Cade smiled at the disgust in her voice before his hand cupped her cheek with a gentleness that made her want to weep.

"I love you, Marigold. Anytime you feel sad or alone or just need a shoulder to cry on, I want you to come to me." He brushed her lips with his. "You're my heart. It kills me to see you hurting."

She leaned into him, wrapping her arms around his neck, feeling his love and his strength. Marigold drew from that strength, and as she stood there in the warm evening breeze with a million stars overhead, she felt herself steady.

For the first time in weeks, her doubts and fears disappeared.

Marigold never did ask Cade about Alice that night. When they'd gotten home, there hadn't been time for talking. She'd wanted him as much as he'd wanted her. When he'd scooped her up and carried her into the bedroom, planting kisses all over her face, she'd embraced the moment.

Now, her husband was on duty, and she had a contract to negotiate.

Charlotte McCray glanced around Muddy Boots. She studied the interior with the intensity of a pawnbroker pricing an object.

She and Marigold sat in a booth of cherry-red vinyl. Cobalt-blue splashes of paint on the white walls simulated rain. On the far wall was a mural of a happy young girl in a raincoat kicking up water.

Though a workday, the iconic café on Main Street was hopping. The calendar might have barely flipped to June, but thanks to the above-average temperatures, tourist season was already in full swing on the peninsula. "The place looks better than I remember."

"Beck and Ami are always looking for ways to update or make improvements to the café. Without changing the feel of the place, of course." Marigold sipped her tea. Coffee was another thing that no longer tasted the same.

Darn fertility drugs, she thought. This newly acquired aversion to wine and coffee hadn't started until after she'd bombarded her body with the drugs.

"I went by Golden Door this morning." Charlotte gave an exaggerated shudder. "It made me sick to see how far it's fallen."

"Well, look who's back." Adam Vogele paused tableside. "When did you blow back into town?"

Charlotte studied the man from beneath lowered lashes for several long seconds.

Tall and rangy, the organic farmer was a handsome guy with dark hair and intense brown eyes. He ran a thriving business, but he hadn't, as far as Marigold knew, been a part of Charlotte's circle of friends.

The admiration for Charlotte in Adam's eyes made perfect sense. With her thick tumble of walnut waves, bright blue eyes and pretty features, Charlotte drew men's glances wherever she went.

What surprised Marigold was that Adam knew Charlotte well enough to stop by the table to chat.

"I'm considering moving back." Charlotte arched a brow. "What do you think?"

"I believe you will do exactly what you want." Though his tone remained easy, Marigold caught an undercurrent of...something. One thing was for certain: These two knew each other a whole lot better than she'd thought.

"You're right." Charlotte gave a little laugh, then waved a dismissive hand. "Good to see you again."

Though astute enough to understand he'd been dismissed, Adam turned to Marigold. "It's good to see you again. Give my regards to Cade."

"I will."

Charlotte watched him stroll off before refocusing her attention on Marigold. "You're married to the sheriff. I don't remember him."

That wasn't surprising since Cade had come to town shortly before Charlotte had moved away. Even when Golden Door had been flourishing, she'd spent more time tending her Chicago salon than she had the one here.

"He's—" Marigold stopped and smiled when she saw Cade emerge from the back room of the café with Beck. Her smile faded when she saw the serious looks on their faces and watched them shake hands. "Right over there."

Charlotte shifted her gaze and studied the two men. "Looks like the conclusion of a business meeting. What would a sheriff have to do with a restaurateur?"

"Beck is also an attorney. When you lived here, he wasn't practicing. He is now and consults with law enforcement...occasionally." *Rarely* was actually more accurate, but Marigold didn't want to open the discussion with Charlotte up to more questions.

This clearly wasn't a social visit. Yet, this morning Cade hadn't mentioned a meeting with his brother-in-law. A hard lump formed in the pit of her stomach, but Marigold managed a smile when the two men headed their way.

Because it had been a while, Marigold performed quick introductions.

"You cut my hair before my sister-in-law came to town," Beck recalled, offering a warm smile.

"I lost a lot of business to the amazing Marigold Bloom." Charlotte smiled, then shifted her gaze to Cade. A look of pure female appreciation filled her bright blue eyes.

If Cade noticed—and how could he not?—it didn't show. He smiled at Marigold as he responded to Charlotte. "She is amazing."

When he leaned over and kissed her briefly on the mouth, Marigold wasn't ashamed to admit her heart swelled. "See you tonight," he said.

"Be safe," she told him, as she did most mornings when he left home for work.

"Nice to meet you, Charlotte."

The woman across from her didn't say a word until the two men were out of earshot. "I always did love a man with broad shoulders and a weapon."

Marigold laughed. "I think it's time to get down to business."

Once their discussion concluded and Charlotte had driven away in her shiny red BMW roadster, Marigold stepped into Book & Cup.

The bookstore, owned by her friend Bea, would be relocating to Wrigley Road at the end of the summer. A move Marigold knew Bea both dreaded and eagerly anticipated.

In September, Bea would become part of the Bloom-Chapin family when she married Clay, Lynn's youngest son.

The bells over the door jingled as she pushed it open. The unexpected scent of blueberries filled the still air.

"I'll be with you—" Bea popped up from beneath the counter. A bright smile lifted her lips. "Marigold. I didn't think I'd see you this morning."

"I was in the neighborhood and thought I'd stop by."

"I'm glad you did." Bea gestured to the coffee machine behind the counter. "Would you like some coffee? Blueberry is the flavor of the day. It's become Clay's new favorite."

Marigold did a momentary self-assessment. As the day progressed, her stomach had felt more settled. She might be able to have some coffee. "I'd love to give it a try."

Only minutes later, they were seated on stools at the counter, each with a mug of steaming coffee before them.

"I thought you'd be busy cutting and curling." Bea cocked her head. "But I'm glad you're here. We didn't get much of a chance to talk last night. There's something I want to ask you."

Marigold sipped her coffee and found it delicious. "What is it?"

"Will you be one of my bridesmaids?" Bea offered an imploring look. "Britt will come back to be my maid of honor."

That, Marigold thought, had been a given. Bea and her twin might be separated by distance right now, but that sisterly bond was a strong one. "How's life in Denver going for her?"

Bea's smile remained on her face. "It's going."

"Did she get her social media job with the Grizzlies?" Marigold couldn't believe she hadn't asked before now. Then again, she'd had a lot on her mind.

"Not yet, but she's still hopeful," Bea continued. "Will you do it?"

She didn't give Marigold a chance to ask if Britt had connected with the team owner's son, JR Driskill, who'd recently been in Good Hope.

"I'd be honored." Marigold met Bea's gaze. "I know I've said it before, but I'm thrilled you'll be part of the family."

Bea's lips curved. "I like to tease Clay that him having a large family was a huge selling point in his favor. With my parents back East and my sister not living here, I like the idea of our children having lots of cousins nearby."

Over the past couple of years, Marigold had plenty of experience keeping a smile on her face when friends and family spoke of getting pregnant. Especially when they seemed to assume that would happen exactly when they wanted it to.

Marigold constantly had to stop herself from warning them that it might not be so easy, that even when you were young and healthy, sometimes there were problems.

Keeping that smile, Marigold inclined her head. "Do you plan to start trying for a family right away?"

"We've discussed it." Bea's smile turned soft and sweet. "For now, I want to enjoy being with Clay. I love him so much. I can't imagine my life without him."

All the way to the salon and all the way home, Bea's words echoed in Marigold's mind. Like Bea, she couldn't imagine her life without the man she loved.

She left the salon early, eagerly anticipating a nap before Cade arrived home at six. The nausea that plagued her off and on was back. She wondered if not eating since her morning meeting with Charlotte had something to do with the queasiness.

Though she loved all of her sisters dearly, the sight of Prim's car in her driveway nearly had her turning and heading the other way. Between the tears and the nausea, she didn't have the energy for a visit.

If Prim hadn't already spotted her and given a welcoming wave, Marigold might have turned or gone on by. Instead, she pulled in beside Prim's minivan and got out.

"Where's the fam?" Marigold asked, not used to seeing her sister without her husband and kids.

"Max took the boys and Adelyn kayaking."

Marigold widened her eyes. "Isn't Adelyn a little young?"

"She's a good listener and loves being out on the water." Prim smiled. "The boys think it's a big deal to have their own kayak. They'll behave and listen, because they know what will happen if they don't."

"Sounds like fun."

Prim narrowed her gaze. "You look tired."

"I'm exhausted." Marigold shrugged. "What else is new?"

She wasn't sure what had brought Prim to her home today, but asking her sister why she was here seemed rude. Marigold had no doubt Prim would tell her in short order.

"Sit." Prim pointed to the porch swing. "I'll get us something to drink while you relax and regroup."

"I have lemonade in the refrigerator as well as sun tea. Help yourself to whatever sounds good."

"What do you want?"

"My stomach has been upset off and on all day. I'll pass on anything for now."

Instead of going inside, Prim took a seat beside Marigold on the swing. She studied her sister for a long moment, no doubt taking note of the dark circles under her eyes and the lines of fatigue etched on her face.

"I've been thinking about you."

"What about me?"

"Your symptoms, for starters."

Marigold lifted her hands. "I'm fine, Prim, really. Please don't worry about me."

"You're my baby sister." The freckles on Prim's face shone like bright pennies in the sunlight. "I love you."

"I love you, too." Marigold blinked furiously as Prim pulled her into an embrace.

"I think you should take a pregnancy test," Prim whispered, her lips against Marigold's hair.

Marigold jerked back. "What are you talking about?"

"Your symptoms are classic, the ones you see in early pregnancy. Just to be sure, I think you should—"

"Prim. Stop." The words came out sharper than she wanted, but Marigold wouldn't apologize. Not this time. Didn't her sister realize that resurrecting this hope, this dream, was hurtful? "I went through years of infertility treatment. Nothing happened. This is simply my body adjusting to being off the hormones."

"What if it's not?" Prim's voice turned pleading. "Take the test. Be sure."

"Sorry. I don't happen to have any pregnancy tests lying around." Marigold's flippant tone hung in the air. "Once that dream died, I got rid of them."

At one time, Marigold had had a dozen such tests in her cupboard. Each time she'd even thought she might be pregnant, she'd taken a test. Not just once, but multiple times. Getting a negative result each time had been emotionally exhausting.

"An accountant is always prepared." Leaning over, Prim opened her purse—a zebra-striped bag the size of Texas—and reached in to pull out a sack. "There are three different tests in here. If you're like me, you'll want to do more than one to confirm the results. Three seemed like a good, solid number."

Prim held out the bag. When Marigold made no move to take it, she heaved a resigned sigh and dropped it on her lap. "You know it's a possibility."

Marigold closed her eyes, struggled against the desire to grab the tests and rush inside.

"I realize there's a possibility," she said at last. "The doctors found a few issues, but nothing that would explain all of our difficulties."

"Then why—?"

"You know why, Prim. You know what it's like to wish for something, but sometimes you have to accept it's not going to happen." Marigold met her sister's gaze. "When Rory was sick, you prayed for him to be healed. It didn't happen. I prayed for a baby. It didn't happen."

"Rory's situation was different. My husband had CF. Yes, I prayed for him to be healed. I wanted him to live so he could continue to be a father to the boys and a husband to me." Prim's eyes grew dark. It was ironic that, in the end it hadn't been CF that had killed Rory, but a rock-climbing accident. "Hope kept us all going during difficult times."

"I still have hope," Marigold admitted. "But now my hope is centered around being picked by a birth mother and her not changing her mind. I thought I'd given up hope of being pregnant. Now, you've raised that hope. That's why what you're asking is so difficult. I don't know if I can bear to see another negative sign on the test stick."

"I understand what you're saying, but you need to do this." Prim's gaze remained firm and direct on Marigold. "If the test is negative, you need to see a doctor and figure out what's going on with all these symptoms you're having."

A chill traveled up Marigold's spine. She'd never considered she might be sick.

"I don't think you're ill." Prim placed a hand on her arm, and Marigold knew she'd read her thoughts. "Take the test."

Marigold gave in to hope and snatched up the sack. "I'll do it. Only because you insist."

"I can come and look at the stick if you don't want to," Prim offered.

"No." Marigold shook her head. "I'm a big girl. I can do it."

In the bathroom, she opened the package that contained the test that was her favorite. Not because it had ever given her the answer she wanted, but for ease of use. She was also familiar with the other two Prim had included.

Minutes later, she stood, transfixed, every fiber of her being focused on the tiny stick in her hand. Instead of the minus sign, which she'd seen more times than she could count, there was a plus.

Her heart pounded, and she swayed slightly, grabbing hold of the sink for support until she steadied. Holding her breath, she brought the stick close and studied it intently. There was no doubt it was a plus.

With trembling hands, she unwrapped the next test. When the word *pregnant* appeared, tears slipped down her cheeks.

How could it be? After all this time and everything they'd been through, how could she be pregnant? Joy flooded her, and she began to sob.

A knock sounded at the door. "Is everything okay?"

"I took the tests," Marigold said, her voice thick with tears.

"May I come in?" Prim asked.

"The door is unlocked."

Prim paused in the doorway, concern furrowing her brow. She glanced at the bathroom vanity top, littered with pregnancy test supplies, before her gaze returned to Marigold's tear-streaked face.

"I'm so sorry, Marigold." Prim took a step forward, though there wasn't much room to spare. "Your symptoms were just so classic that—"

"I'm pregnant." Marigold pushed the words she'd longed to say for years past frozen lips. She gestured to the vanity. "Two tests. I did two tests. They both gave the same result."

Prim studied the sticks Marigold had arranged on the vanity. A smile slowly blossomed on her lips, and she lunged forward, wrapping her arms around her sister.

"Congratulations. I'm so happy for you and Cade."

"I'm so happy, too." Marigold laughed and hugged her sister tight. "I can't believe it. I just can't believe it."

"Well, I'm going to head home." Prim smiled. "I can't wait to hear Cade's reaction when you tell him."

Though happiness flowed through Marigold's veins like

warm honey, she still found herself unable to fully embrace the idea. She gripped her sister's arm. "Promise you won't tell anyone, not even Max, until I give the go-ahead?"

Prim frowned. "Why?"

"I want to tell Cade, then I want to see a doctor. Once the pregnancy is confirmed, we'll tell the family."

Prim's gaze searched hers. "You're still not convinced."

"I'm ninety percent convinced," Marigold told her sister. "I want to be a hundred percent before sharing the news with the world."

Prim smiled. "It's such wonderful news."

"You'll keep it on the down low for now?"

"My lips are," Prim mimed zipping her lips shut, "sealed."

CHAPTER FOUR

Cade couldn't wait for a quiet evening at home with his wife. Especially since Marigold had called that afternoon and told him she was planning on grilling salmon, a personal favorite of his.

Things had been rough between him and Marigold lately, and that was his fault. Granted, she'd been moody and weepy, but that was to be expected considering the heavy-duty drugs she'd been on.

His unexpected trips to Milwaukee and the overheard phone conversation with Alice hadn't helped. He knew Marigold worried about his relationship with his former fiancée. And he hadn't been able to dispel her fears. That would mean telling her exactly why he was texting and talking and visiting Alice.

Maybe he would stop and get Marigold flowers on the way home. He pulled open the door to his truck and considered. Stopping by the General Store would add an extra ten minutes to his trip, but it'd be worth it to see a smile light up Marigold's face.

His phone rang just as the truck's engine roared to life. "This is Cade."

"Cade. It's Alice. I have news."

He waited a second for the Bluetooth to kick in and for her

voice to come through the speakers in the truck. "What kind of news?"

"Nina wants to meet you." Alice's voice shook with excitement. "She's narrowed it down to two couples. You and Marigold made the finals."

"When?"

"Tonight if you can make it."

Cade's mind raced.

"I'll swing by and pick up Marigold." He did the quick calculation in his head. "Depending on traffic, it'll take a good three hours for us to get there. Will that work?"

"I guess I wasn't clear." Alice cleared her throat. "She wants to meet you first. Alone. Then, if you're acceptable, she will meet with both of you."

Cade frowned. "That doesn't make sense."

"Sometimes things in independent adoptions don't make sense." Alice's voice gentled. "Nina's baby is due in three weeks. She knows it's a boy. Her father was a detective. Her grandfather a US marshal. Service runs in her family. It's important to her to have her son grow up in a law enforcement family."

Clay knew the birth father was out of the picture and had relinquished his parental rights. "If family is so important, why hasn't she told her family she's pregnant?"

"She says they'll try to talk her out of adoption, and she doesn't want the extra hassle. Her words, not mine. Nina strongly feels adoption is the best option for her and the baby."

Cade hoped that when he had a child, that boy or girl would always feel like they could confide in him. But he didn't know Nina's parents, and she was twenty-one. This was her decision to make.

"It's not uncommon for a birth mother to not tell her family," Alice said into the lengthening silence. "But it's not as common as you might think."

Alice had left her Detroit law practice to move to Milwaukee to work in a firm that specialized in private adoptions.

When he and Marigold had run into Alice, she'd mentioned her new position in passing. At that point, Marigold had already left for the concession stands. Cade had told Alice he and Marigold had been screened and approved by an agency, but had been warned the wait might be long.

Alice wanted to help. When she contacted him, he'd given her the information she requested and told her to keep a lookout. A couple of weeks ago, she'd contacted him about Nina.

A senior at Marquette University in Milwaukee, with everything in place to attend law school in Chicago in the fall, Nina had said a baby didn't fit into her plans. She could have gone with an agency, but a friend of a friend's father worked for Alice's law firm.

In addition to wanting the father to be someone with a law enforcement background, she preferred a couple who already had at least one child. Apparently, Nina was an only child, so she wanted her son to have siblings.

Alice had confided that the other couple met both criteria. He and Marigold met only one. Another reason he hadn't wanted to get Marigold's hopes up.

Nina's plan was to have the baby, sign the adoption papers and move to Chicago. He wanted to wait until he was certain they stood a real chance at adopting this baby before saying anything to his wife.

"If you pass muster, she'll meet Marigold." Excitement filled Alice's voice. "Depending on what she decides, you could have a baby by Independence Day."

"I'm on my way."

He'd meet with Nina tonight.

Once he got home after the meeting, he'd tell Marigold everything.

~

Hours earlier, Marigold had stowed the salmon and spears of asparagus in the refrigerator. She'd snuffed out the candles that had been on the table, then put away the linen tablecloth.

Her celebration had fallen apart the second Cade had called. Instead of coming home, he was already on his way to Milwaukee.

Though stunned, she'd had enough sense to ask if he'd be seeing Alice. His momentary hesitation had told her all she needed to know.

"Safe trip," she told him, not able at that moment to think of anything else to say.

"We'll talk when I get home." There was a long pause. "Or tomorrow. It might be late tonight."

"Whatever."

"Marigold." His voice was quiet and intense. "There's so much I need to say."

"Okay." She closed her eyes and forced herself to breathe.

"You said you have something to tell me."

"It can wait." She pressed her hand against her flat belly and felt tears sting the backs of her eyes. She almost added, *It isn't important*, but the words died on her tongue.

What she had to tell him *was* important.

Now, they had a baby to discuss, plus whatever was going on between him and Alice.

"Tell me something, Cade."

"Sure."

"Are you and Alice getting back together?"

"Are you kidding? No." The shock in his voice rang true. "That's not what's happening at all."

"Then why are you seeing her?"

"I'll explain everything when I get back." His voice was fierce.

"But I can tell you that there is no woman in this world I love the way I love you."

∾

Keeping this from Marigold had been a mistake. In all their married life, he'd never kept anything from her. Their relationship was built on honesty and trust. Now, he'd rocked that foundation with his desire to protect her from more heartbreak.

That ended tonight. Regardless of how things went with Nina, he would tell his wife everything when he got home.

His mind conjured up all sorts of scenarios on the long drive to Milwaukee. Like Marigold, he'd come to expect disappointment.

Cade told himself that if it didn't work out tonight with Nina, it wasn't meant to be. The office building that housed the law offices was quiet as a tomb. It had good security. He'd had to call Alice to come down and let him in.

Alice smiled as she unlocked the door. She was an attractive woman with a confident manner and a ready smile. His reaction to being around her had only confirmed what he'd already known. Marrying her would have been a mistake. There was only one woman he was meant to be with, and she was waiting at home for him.

"How is Nina?" Cade asked on the elevator ride to the tenth floor.

"She's an amazing young woman." Alice's voice rang with approval. "Loads of ambition. She'll be very successful one day."

Success had always been important to Alice. Important enough that she'd urged him not to endanger his own career by reporting fellow cops who were dirty.

He'd followed his conscience, and that had ended their relationship. He'd realized in the years since that they'd been on shaky ground prior to that defining incident.

"I was asking more about her feelings regarding the baby. The birth is close. Do you see her having second thoughts?"

Surprise flickered across Alice's face. "Not at all. She's very driven. Reminds me of myself at that age."

"It's a big decision."

Alice placed a hand on his arm. "I don't see her changing her mind. The only question up in the air right now is if you and Marigold will be her choice."

As Cade sat across from the young woman, he told himself he had to trust that whatever Nina decided would be the right decision for her and for him and Marigold.

"After serving in the Marines, I was on the police force in Detroit for a number of years," Cade told the girl, who looked impossibly young, her blond hair pulled back in a tail. "I started out as an officer, eventually received my detective's shield. I enjoyed the work, but eventually wanted something different. I'm now the sheriff in Good Hope, Wisconsin. It's a small community on the Door County peninsula."

"Big city to small town." Nina's blue eyes narrowed, and her gaze turned speculative. "Quite a change."

"Best move I ever made." Cade smiled. "I get to do the work I love, but have time for family and friends. Good Hope is an amazing community. My wife has a lot of family there, and—"

"I want to hear more about your service record," Nina interrupted. "If I decide to move forward, your wife can tell me more about her family and the community. Why did you leave Detroit? Did you do something wrong? Were you in danger of being kicked off the force?"

Cade met her gaze. Normally, he didn't speak of that time. But the arrests and convictions were public record, and he sensed Nina wouldn't accept any evasion. "I discovered several officers in my unit had failed to log into evidence money and drugs seized during searches of homes. I turned them in to Internal Affairs. They were eventually indicted and convicted."

"What about the thin blue line?" Nina asked pointedly.

Even if he hadn't known, the question told him there was a cop in her family.

He kept his gaze on her face. "The thin blue line breaks for dirty cops."

"I bet not everyone saw it that way."

Cade resisted the urge to glance at Alice. He shrugged. "I had to follow my own conscience."

"My father and granddad would agree with you on that." Nina shifted in her chair and winced, a hand moving to her back.

"Are you okay?" Cade asked.

When he started to rise to his feet, she waved him down.

"This last month, I've been having a lot of what's called Braxton Hicks contractions. False labor pains." Nina took a breath, then relaxed. "Over for now."

"What other questions can I answer for you?" Cade asked. "Or if you'd prefer to wait until you feel better, I can come back."

"Thanks." The tightness around her mouth eased. "I appreciate your concern and you meeting with me on such short notice. But I've put off this decision too long already."

That's what had Cade worried. "Are you considering keeping the baby?"

Shock flickered across her face. "Absolutely not. He deserves parents who can give him time and attention. Both things are in short supply in my life."

"We'd give him a good home," Cade told her. "One filled with love. I grew up with three brothers, so I know boys. My wife is one of four girls, but—"

"When can I meet her?"

"Name the time and place. We'll be there."

"Tomorrow at ten?" Nina glanced at Alice. "We need to get moving on this."

"I'm available then," Alice told her.

Pushing back her chair, Nina stood.

Cade rounded the table and held out his hand. She was only an inch or two taller than Marigold and possessed a cool composure he wouldn't have expected in one so young.

"It was a pleasure meeting you, Nina."

The hand that closed over his was ice-cold.

Not as steady as she appeared, he thought.

"I look forward to meeting your wife."

"You'll love her." His voice warmed the way it did each time he mentioned Marigold. "She's an amazing woman."

Marigold's heart began to pound when she heard the garage door lift. She glanced at her phone. Two in the morning. Anger warred with the fear that had gripped her as the hours ticked slowly by.

What had Cade been doing?

She thought of the salmon and asparagus. Of the coconut lime sherbet in the freezer that was Cade's favorite. And of the bottle of sparkling cider.

Somewhere around eleven o'clock, anger and hurt and a dozen other emotions that were so tangled together she didn't know how to separate one from the other had peaked in a righteous fury.

Then she came to her senses.

Cade loved her. That's what he'd said. That's what she believed. She would trust him. For now.

Marigold looked up when her husband walked into the living room. She had dimmed the lights and was sitting on the sofa, sipping a glass of cider. She'd changed from the pretty dress she'd had on earlier into the bright pink silk pj's he'd given her for Christmas.

"Sorry I'm so late." He raked a hand through his hair and plopped down on the other end of the sofa. "It's been a long day."

He looked tired, she thought, and stressed, with little lines etched deep around his eyes.

"For me, too," she said.

"You didn't have to wait up." His eyes met hers. "But I'm really glad you did."

It was an opening, and she stepped through, somehow even managed to offer a tentative smile. "Why don't you tell me what's going on?"

Cade took a deep breath, let it out slowly. The serious look on his face had her body going rigid.

"Alice has found us a birth mother who is due in the next month. She's down to two couples, and we're one of them."

Marigold felt her heart leap, the same way it had when she'd seen the plus sign on the stick. "Why is this the first I'm hearing about this?"

"Her father and grandfather are in law enforcement, and Nina —that's the birth mother—wants an adoptive father with ties to law enforcement. Her other preference is that the couple have another child. Apparently, Nina is an only child who's always wished for a sibling." Cade blew out another breath. "Alice hopes she'll make an exception once she meets you."

"So…Alice handles adoptions at her firm." Marigold spoke slowly as the puzzle pieces began falling into place. "Did she want you to keep this from me?"

"No." Cade expelled yet another heavy breath. "That bad idea was totally my own."

"How could you think it was a good idea?" While the other puzzle pieces were fitting nicely together, this one stuck out.

"We've been through so many disappointments. You said you didn't think you could handle another one right now." Cade scooted over and took her hands in his.

A little of the tightness of her body released at his touch. The coldness inside her began to warm as she realized the truth of his words.

"We don't meet one of this young woman's two criteria, and moving forward depended on the meeting I had with her this evening."

"How did it go?" Marigold asked.

"It went well, I think. She wants to meet with us both at ten a.m. tomorrow." His words came quickly now. "I realize it's short notice, and you'll probably have to cancel a million appointments, but Alice believes we have a real chance."

Before she could speak, his hands tightened on hers. "If things go well tomorrow, we could be the parents of a baby boy by the end of the month."

"You really think that's a possibility?"

"She liked me. Or rather, I didn't blow it, so yes, I think it could happen."

Cade studied her face for a long time, and she saw the puzzlement in his eyes.

"You don't seem as excited as I thought you'd be," he said carefully, as if searching for footing on unfamiliar terrain.

"I am excited," she told him, meaning every word. "It's just I have a wrinkle to toss into the mix."

While it was an amazing wrinkle, and one she knew he'd love, it was definitely unexpected. Her heart began to pound an erratic rhythm.

Marigold thought of her sister Fin, who'd recently learned she was pregnant again after giving birth to her first child about four months earlier. She hadn't understood why Fin and Jeremy had deliberately waited to share their news with the family.

Fin's claim of being in shock hadn't rung true to her. Now, Marigold understood. The idea of having two children under the age of one was a heady, yet also frightening, thought.

"What kind of wrinkle?" His voice hitched. "Are you ill?"

For a second, she wondered why he'd be concerned she was sick. Until she remembered her symptoms over the past month. Ones that now made perfect sense.

"I'm not ill, Cade." Marigold fixed her eyes on his. "I'm pregnant."

He blinked. Her lawman, a guy who caught on to everything so quickly it usually made her head spin, appeared to be having difficulty processing her words. "Pregnant?"

"Yes." She smiled and pulled his hand to her belly. "You and I are having a baby."

Tears filled his eyes. "A baby?"

Marigold nodded, the lump in her throat making speech impossible.

"I can't believe it." He let out a whoop, took her in his arms and spun her around.

When he stopped, she closed her eyes and held him tight.

He stilled. "Is that what you wanted to tell me tonight?"

She nodded, her head still buried in the crook of his neck.

"I ruined it for you."

"You didn't ruin anything." She raised her head and looked into his eyes. "You were simply busy doing your part to expand our family."

"Would you still want to go forward with an adoption?" He brushed the curls back from her face. "If Nina chooses us, we'd have two little ones."

"Two babies to love," Marigold told him. "We want a big family. We'd be off to a most excellent start."

"Have I told you lately how much I love you?"

She pulled him to her with a fierceness that surprised them both. "I feel horrible for doubting you for even one second."

"I should have told you everything from the start. Keeping things from each other isn't our way." He kissed the top of her head. "It won't happen again."

"Good." She smiled and pulled back. "It's time we got to bed."

"You're right. You need your sleep." He stood and pulled her to her feet. "I still can't believe it."

"The pregnancy explains so much. The symptoms I've been having are classic, but I didn't make the connection."

Without warning, he wrapped his arms around her and once again spun her around. She was laughing by the time they came to a stop. "What was that about?"

Joy filled his eyes. "Celebrating this most momentous occasion."

"I have another way we can celebrate." She smiled. "I'll give you a hint. It involves getting naked."

CHAPTER FIVE

Marigold glanced at the time on the dash as she slid into the passenger seat of Cade's truck. They'd allowed themselves three and a half hours for the drive to Milwaukee.

With the sun up and the sky clear, it should be smooth sailing all the way. Marigold had gotten together snacks for them to munch on as well as bottles of water. Cade had brought a huge travel mug of coffee as well.

The city limit sign for Good Hope was in their rearview when her phone pinged with a text.

"I thought Charlotte and I had everything settled," she told Cade with a puzzled frown.

Though annoyed at being awakened at six a.m., Charlotte had agreed to contact Marigold's customers about the change in plans for the day. If they were willing, she'd fill in. Otherwise, Charlotte would reschedule their appointments with Marigold.

When Marigold retrieved her phone from her purse, it wasn't Charlotte's name on the readout. A shiver of unease slithered up her spine at the sight of David Chapin's name.

"The text is from David," she told Cade. "It's a group text."

"What's does it say?"

Marigold's heart stopped. Just stopped. Nononono, she thought. This couldn't be happening.

"Marigold?" Cade's voice remained soft and low, as if he sensed her distress. "What's wrong?"

"We have to go to the hospital in Sturgeon."

"Okay. We're not far." He veered off the highway in the direction of the hospital. "Tell me what's happened."

"It's my dad. Lynn called 911. Possible heart attack." Tears slipped down Marigold's cheeks. "I can't lose him, Cade. Not my dad."

"You won't." Reaching over, Cade clasped Marigold's hand. "Did you know that ninety percent of people who have a heart attack survive?"

"I didn't, but I'm glad to hear it."

Cade pulled into the Emergency parking lot. He'd barely stopped when Marigold flung open her door. She was at the sliding doors leading into the ER by the time he unbuckled his seat belt.

The red-headed nurse at the desk looked up when she rushed to the counter. "My dad, Steve Bloom, came in—"

"Marigold."

She whirled at the sound of her name. Seconds later, she was clamping her fingers around David's forearms. "Where is he? Where's my dad?"

"The second the ambulance arrived," David told her, "they took him back. They'd already started an IV and hooked him up to a heart monitor en route."

"They insisted we stay out here." Frustration filled Lynn's voice. "They wouldn't let me go back with him."

Without makeup and wearing cotton pants and a simple tee, Lynn looked every day of her sixty years. But there was a fierceness to her expression and a resolve in her voice that told Marigold no one was going to push her around.

Marigold lightly touched Lynn's arm. "Can you tell me what happened?"

Before Lynn had a chance to respond, the doors to the ER slid open, and her sisters rushed in. Their husbands weren't with them, which told Marigold they'd stayed home with the children. Except for Fin. Jeremy held Eddie as Fin joined her siblings, who quickly surrounded Lynn.

"Where's Dad?" Fin demanded.

"How's he doing?" Prim asked.

"I want to see him," Ami insisted.

The doors opened again, and Lynn's other two children, Clay and Greer, joined the group. Wyatt, Greer's husband, paused to speak with Cade.

As the waiting room was otherwise deserted, there was no need for Lynn to keep her voice down.

"Before bed, Steve complained he just didn't feel right." Lynn's voice trembled slightly before she steadied it. "He thought it might be something he ate, but we'd had the same dinner, and I felt fine."

Lynn closed her eyes, her fingers tightly curled together.

"What happened then," Fin demanded, rather than asked.

"Is that when you called 911?" Prim offered Lynn an encouraging smile and shot Fin a warning glance.

Fin was worried—heck, they all were—but when Delphinium Rakes got worried, she pushed and pushed hard.

The trouble was, as strong as Lynn was, right now she looked as if she was on the verge of breaking.

"He woke me up at six, and he was nauseous. He said he was having pain in his chest." Lynn's voice hitched. "It reminded me of Robert."

"Steve said no, this wasn't a heart attack. He told me he was going to take an antacid and go back to bed." Lynn's jaw set in a tight line. "I called 911 and insisted he chew an aspirin while we waited."

"Bet he loved that." Ami managed a chuckle.

"He wasn't happy. I didn't care. I wasn't taking any chances." Her lips pressed together for several seconds. "I only regret not bringing him in before we went to bed."

"You couldn't have known things would get worse." David put a hand on his mother's shoulders. "You did all the right things, Mom. He's in good hands now."

"They have an excellent cardiology program here." Jeremy spoke for the first time. "When they were talking about my grandmother having heart surgery, we did our research."

"What was that doctor's name?" Prim asked him. "The one who took care of your grandmother?"

"Nolan Passmore," Jeremy told her.

"I don't know who is taking care of Steve." Lynn pushed to her feet. "But I'm going to find out."

While Lynn was doing her thing, Cade motioned to Marigold, and they stepped to the side.

"What is it?" she asked, casting sideways glances at Lynn, who appeared to be in a deep discussion with the nurse.

"I'm going to text Alice and cancel the meeting."

Marigold stared blankly at him.

"The ten o'clock with Nina?" he prompted.

"Oh yeah, that." Her gaze once again slid to Lynn. "Yes, go ahead and cancel. There's no way I can leave my dad."

"I agree. We need to be here." He bent over and kissed the top of her head, then pulled out his phone.

"You could still go."

He shook his head. "Today was for her to meet you. Besides, I'm not leaving you."

Marigold gripped his hand. "I'm glad."

"I love him, too." Cade pulled her close. "It's going to be okay."

She expelled a breath. "Nina will probably pick the other couple if we don't show."

Cade thought of the young woman he'd met. "Probably."

"I guess that's the way it has to be." Marigold rested her head against Cade's chest. "I can't leave my dad."

Four hours later, after a plethora of tests, Steve was in the operating room. But not for his heart.

"The doctors said he can go home in the morning," Lynn told the assembled brood. "Apparently, laparoscopic removal of a gall-bladder isn't all that big of a deal."

"Except probably to the guy having it done," Beck quipped, making them all laugh.

Once the spouses had found sitters, they'd also gathered at the hospital. Pastor Marshall had arrived, as well as other close friends of Steve and the family.

"Let's take a walk down the hall." Marigold looked up at Cade, and in answer, he took her hand.

"You look tired," he told her once they were out of earshot of the others.

"I am tired, but so relieved." Her big blue eyes met his. "Hearing this was just his gallbladder and not his heart…"

"Beck is right, a gallbladder attack is serious, but—"

"—not on the level of a heart attack," Marigold finished.

"Exactly," Cade agreed. "Definitely not of the same magnitude as a heart attack."

"I'm glad Lynn was with him and that she acted quickly." Marigold's lower lip trembled. "While she was relaying what led up to her calling 911, all I could think of was what if dad was still living alone? Something could have happened to him, and none of us would have known."

"Well, he doesn't live alone anymore. The doctors are confi-dent he'll make a full recovery."

She paused for a long moment. Cade knew his wife well enough to know she had something to say.

"I'm sorry about missing the appointment with Nina." She expelled a breath. "We'd have been fabulous parents to her little boy."

"Staying was the right decision," Cade told her. "Besides, I firmly adhere to the philosophy that if it's meant to be, it will happen."

∽

An email from Alice later that day, right around the time Marigold's dad was being discharged, appeared to confirm their fears. Nina had moved on to interviewing the other couple.

Though disappointed, Marigold had her spirits buoyed by a visit to the doctor that week that confirmed she was six weeks pregnant and due shortly after the first of the year. Though she yearned to shout out the news, she was determined to tell the entire family at one time.

This meant waiting until Sunday when her father was feeling more like his normal self.

"Prim told me she's ready to burst with holding in the news," Marigold confided to Cade when he arrived home from work on Thursday.

"I feel that way myself." He grinned. "Remember when you once said when we got the news we'd be shouting it from the top of Eagle Tower? That's exactly what I want to do."

"Sunday," she promised, curving her fingers around his.

She smiled when he pulled her in for a kiss.

An after-dinner text from Alice caught them both off guard.

Marigold read it twice on Cade's phone, then glanced up at him. "What do you think this means?"

"If I had to hazard a guess, I'd say Nina's second-choice couple didn't wow her." He cocked his head. "Tomorrow is a busy day for you. We could ask for a delay."

Marigold shook her head. "I'd like to meet her. And if the baby is due any day now, she's running out of time, too."

"What about your appointments?"

"I'll put in longer hours on Saturday, maybe work a few hours on Sunday." Marigold smiled. "I'll give them the choice of rescheduling or seeing Charlotte."

"Is Charlotte available?"

Marigold composed a quick text to Charlotte. "I'm about to find out."

~

"You don't seem nervous." Cade spoke in a low voice as they waited to be ushered into the law firm's conference room.

"I'm not." Marigold met his gaze. "I'll answer her questions honestly. Either we'll be the couple she wants, or we won't."

"How'd you get so Zen?" he asked, his tone clearly admiring.

"I don't know. Maybe it was worrying about my dad that put everything into focus for me. You and I are blessed, Cade. With family, with friends who love us and we love in return. Most of all with each other."

She stopped when Alice opened the door and motioned them into the conference room. "Please come in."

Nina stood by the shiny oval table, her gaze sharp and assessing.

"Nina, it's good to see you again." Cade spoke before Alice had a chance. "This is my wife, Marigold."

Marigold knew Nina was twenty-one, but with her long blond hair pulled back from her face with a paisley headband and the bright blue maternity shirt that clung to her large belly, she looked much younger. Except for the gleam in her eyes. "Marigold. That's an odd name."

"My sisters and I all have flower names, so it seems totally normal to me." Marigold kept her tone easy. "Before I married

Cade, my last name was Bloom. I always thought Marigold Bloom had a nice ring."

"Please, have a seat." Alice gestured Marigold and Cade to two seats across the table from her and Nina. "Can I get you anything to drink? Water? Coffee?"

Marigold looked at Cade, then shook her head. "We're fine."

"I was sorry you had to cancel the last meeting," Alice said.

"Someone was ill?" Nina inclined her head.

Marigold didn't doubt Alice had told the young woman the reason for the last-minute cancellation, but she played along.

"We were on our way to Milwaukee when we got word my father had been taken to the hospital by ambulance. At the time, we thought he'd had a heart attack." Just saying the words brought memories flooding back and had Marigold's heart rate jumping.

"Is he doing okay?" Sympathy filled Nina's eyes, as if she felt Marigold's pain.

"He is. Thank you for asking." Marigold took Cade's hand. "The pain actually came from his gallbladder. He ended up having it out the same day."

Nina's gaze lingered for a moment on their joined hands. "I have some questions for you, if you don't mind answering."

"That's why I'm here." Marigold paused. "Before we get started, there's something we need to tell you. It's an update on the information we put down on the form."

"What is it?"

"Everything should have been on the original application." Clearly not pleased, Alice shot Cade a censuring glance. "I stressed that repeatedly."

He only smiled back.

"We discovered we're pregnant." Marigold met Nina's surprised glance with a steady look of her own. "Our baby is due shortly after the first of the year."

"You're no longer interested in adoption." Disappointment flooded Alice's voice.

"We are still very much interested," Marigold assured her. "We just wanted to share that our circumstances have changed. We don't want you to feel we held anything back."

Nina studied her for a long minute. "I appreciate it."

"Nina, if you feel this development changes anything, we can—"

The young woman lifted a hand, shutting down Alice. "Tell me about your family."

Marigold relaxed against the back of her chair. "You might regret leaving that request so open-ended. I can talk about my family all day."

"I'll let you know when I've heard enough."

Cade sat back in his chair. "Hey, Alice, does that coffee offer still stand?"

CHAPTER SIX

Cade was on his second cup, and Marigold had just finished describing her three sisters and discussing their family get-togethers.

"You have lots of nieces and nephews," Nina mused, tapping a nail against the tabletop. "Is your family supportive of adoption?"

"Very supportive." Marigold smiled. "My stepbrother David's oldest child was adopted as an infant through a private agency."

"Do they have other children?"

Marigold nodded. "He and his wife recently had a baby boy. His name is Carter. So your child would have—"

"They had a baby of their own?" Nina appeared determined to press the point.

"Brynn is their own. As is Carter." Marigold's tone turned cool. "By blood or by heart, Brynn and Carter are both their children. If you choose us, your son will be ours as much as any child I give birth to."

"Would you let him know about me?"

"Whatever you want him to know. I'm hoping," Marigold glanced at Cade, "we could at least give him the basics about you."

"You wouldn't keep the fact that he's adopted from him?"

Shock skittered across Marigold's face. "Of course not. We chose to have him. We'd want him to know he is the child of our heart. Keeping his adoption from him would be starting our life together with a lie."

"Your son would have our love," Cade told her. "And our attention."

"Even with a new baby coming?"

"My sister has a four-month-old, and her second child is due before that baby will be a year old." Marigold smiled. "If Fin can do it, so can I. It'll be a busy time, but an exciting one. My sisters and I are close in age. There are advantages to spacing them out and advantages to having two children close together."

"You've built quite a reputation as a hairstylist." Nina cocked her head. "Do you plan to continue to work?"

"I do. I plan on cutting back my hours, but I'll continue to grow my business. I enjoy what I do, and I'm good at it." Marigold shrugged. "Right now, I'm in the process of bringing in a partner of sorts. A lot depends on how she works out and how things go with two babies. I won't neglect my husband or my children."

"Marigold won't be flying solo." Cade set down his coffee cup. "We will both parent our children. My job gives me a certain amount of flexibility, and I plan to take full advantage. I want Marigold happy, too. I won't neglect my wife or my children."

Nina gave a nod, then winced.

"More Braxton Hicks?" Alice asked, her brows furrowed in concern.

"I don't think so." Nina gripped the edge of the table so hard her fingers turned white. "I've been having contractions off and on. They're more frequent now and a whole lot harder."

"You're in labor?" Alice jumped up. "We need to get you to the hospital."

"Yes," Marigold agreed as she and Cade pushed back their chairs and stood. "We can continue this another time."

"There's no need to meet again," Nina told them between gritted teeth.

Cade wrapped an arm around Marigold's shoulders. Though she gave no outward evidence of her disappointment, he felt her trembling. "Well, thank you anyway. We appreciate you considering us."

Marigold shot the woman a warm smile. "I understand you have to make the decision that is right for you and your son."

"*Your* son," Nina said pointedly.

Marigold looked up at Cade.

His gaze returned to Nina. "Are you saying..."

"I'm saying that I pick you and Marigold. The life you have in Good Hope, the family connections and the love you share are everything I want for my son."

"What about the other couple?" Alice asked. "You were impressed. Don't you want to think about this a little longer?"

"I don't have time, and anyway, my decision is final." Nina met Marigold's gaze. "The other couple has a five-year-old, so they were a good fit, too, but I like the idea of this baby growing up with a sibling close in age. And the two of you are so good together."

"Thank you." Marigold rounded the table. "You won't be sorry."

Alice's gaze shifted from the two women to him. "I'll finish getting the papers drawn up right away."

Marigold winced as Nina gripped her hands hard. A second later, liquid pooled on the hardwood floor at their feet.

After the pain passed, Nina stared down in disbelief. In that instant, her controlled demeanor slipped, and she looked like a girl scared out of her mind. "My water broke."

"You'll be okay." Marigold offered a reassuring smile. "This is all normal."

"How long have you been having contractions?" Cade kept his

tone matter-of-fact, as if ruptured membranes were an everyday occurrence in his world.

"Since last night," Nina told him. "All the books I've read say that in a first pregnancy, labor can take days. It's not like it is in the movies." Nina leaned against the table, appearing on the verge of tears. "They've really picked up in the last couple of hours."

"You're doing amazing." Marigold stood in front of Nina and placed her hands on the girl's shoulders. "Everything is going to be fine."

"This isn't how I imagined it." Nina's lips trembled. She glanced at Alice. "I'm sorry about the mess."

"No worries. We're going to get you to the hospital." With her lips pressed tightly together, Alice snatched up her purse and ushered them out of the conference room. "I've never delivered a baby and don't intend to start now."

Even before they reached the outer offices, the force of another contraction had Nina doubling over and gripping her belly. "He's coming."

From the closeness of the contractions, Cade knew they wouldn't make it to a hospital.

"I can't do this alone," Nina wailed.

"You're not alone." Marigold's calm voice and gentle smile offered reassurance. "We're not going anywhere. And you've got an expert right here with you. My husband has delivered plenty of babies."

Two deliveries didn't exactly qualify as *plenty*, but Cade wasn't about to argue the point.

"Call for an ambulance," he told Alice. "This baby isn't going to wait."

Horror had Alice's mouth going wide. "You can't deliver a baby here."

"Either that or in the car." He kept his tone matter-of-fact. "I vote for here."

Cade found a spot on the sofa in Alice's office for the delivery, while Alice scurried around in search of requested supplies.

Marigold held Nina's hand and offered words of encouragement through contractions that came with increasing frequency.

Cade had delivered two babies. He knew the drill.

But this time was profoundly different.

Fifteen minutes later, when his firstborn son slid into his hands, wailing loudly with tiny arms flailing, Cade felt tears sting his eyes, and his vision blurred. He glanced around and discovered he wasn't the only one overcome with emotion.

Tears slipped down his wife's cheeks as she gazed at the precious newborn. Not just any infant. Their child. Their son.

The baby was a healthy shade of pink and had a lusty cry and a head as bald as a billiard ball.

After wiping his nose and mouth and making sure his airways were clear, Cade gently wrapped him in the soft towel Alice offered.

When he started to lay the child on Nina's chest, she held up a hand.

"No." Nina shifted her gaze to Marigold. "His mother needs to hold him first."

Marigold sniffled, swiped at her wet cheeks and offered Nina a tremulous smile.

"Let's make sure you're nice and warm first." Taking the shawl from Alice, Marigold tucked the soft garment around Nina. With great gentleness, she brushed a lock of damp hair back from the young woman's cheek. "You did good."

"Thank you," Nina whispered in a voice choked with emotion.

"We're the ones who should be thanking you. You've given us a wondrous gift." Marigold gave Nina's hand another squeeze before holding out her arms for the baby.

Once she held him—and had anything ever looked so right?— Cade slipped an arm around Marigold's shoulders. Together, they studied the sweet face with the tiny nose and rosebud mouth.

"I love him already." Marigold spoke in a reverent whisper.

"I know." Cade had to clear his throat before he could say more. "I feel the same."

"He'll have a wonderful life with us," Marigold assured Nina.

"What happens now?" Cade asked Alice after the EMTs arrived and loaded Nina and the baby on the gurney.

"I'll finish drawing up the papers and meet you at the hospital to sign then." Alice's tone had turned all business. "Once the doctor feels the baby is ready to be dismissed, you can take him home."

The three rode the elevator down with Nina and the baby. They'd nearly reached the main floor when Alice turned to Cade and Marigold. "Thirty days after the judge signs the order terminating Nina's parental rights, he'll be yours. Unless she changes her mind."

The finger stroking the baby's cheek stopped. Nina looked up and shook her head. "I won't change my mind."

The certainty in her voice reassured Marigold.

Nina's gaze shifted to Cade and then to Marigold. "You're his parents now. What are you going to call him?"

Marigold glanced at Cade. They'd discussed names on the drive to Milwaukee. Had that been only hours ago?

"We thought we'd call him Caleb." Marigold smiled. "The name has several meanings. One of them is heart. It seemed fitting, as he's our child, not by blood, but by heart."

"I love the name you've chosen for your son." Nina glanced down at the baby sleeping on her chest. "You're going to have a wonderful life, Caleb Rallis. Your parents will see to it."

～

The bright June sun had Marigold grabbing a hat for Caleb before they left the house. The past three weeks had been a whirlwind. She and Cade had brought their son home, announced they'd be welcoming another baby in January and moved into the Dunlevey mansion.

With so many changes occurring in such a short time, she and Cade had truly needed a village. Their village—her family and the people of Good Hope—had sprung into action without being asked.

They'd packed, cleaned and moved boxes and furniture. They'd filled Marigold and Cade's nursery with everything a baby needed. Even Marigold's customers had stepped up and graciously accepted Charlotte as a temporary fill-in.

Marigold glanced down at the baby strapped to her chest, his head now covered in the blue cotton hat. Through the fabric of the Moby Wrap binding him to her, she gently stroked his back. "Before you came into my life, I didn't know one little baby could be so much work. Even knowing what I know now, I wouldn't change a thing."

"I agree with both statements." Cade strode across the kitchen, kissed them both. "I'm bummed I can't make the shower."

"The plans are for it to be more of an open-house type of thing. So, while you're patrolling the streets of Good Hope, if you happen to find yourself driving past my sister's house..." Marigold gazed up at Cade through lowered lashes. "You might feel the need to stop and make sure there's no criminal mischief occurring."

The baby shower, held at Ami's house but hosted by the entire family, was long overdue. With everything happening so quickly, there hadn't been time before now to fit one in.

"Criminal mischief?" He rubbed his chin. "If that's a possibility, I'll definitely stop by."

"Your son and I are heading there now." She flashed a smile. "Hope to see you soon."

Since her sister lived close, Marigold decided to walk. The warm air held the clean, fresh scent of spring. Red, white and blue flags with images of exploding fireworks hung from ornate light poles and fluttered in the breeze.

With her palm flat against Caleb's back, Marigold paused in front of Kyle and Eliza Kendrick's home to study the festive decorations. She made a mental note to speak with Cade about getting some patriotic bunting for the railing on their porch.

Her gaze lingered on the flowers edging the slate walkway leading around the house. Impressed, Marigold decided she'd stop by the Garden of Eden later today and grab some annuals.

The red-and-white-striped ivy geraniums in hanging baskets had just captured her attention when a hand touched her arm.

Marigold whirled. The sudden motion had Caleb's eyes popping open.

"They're called candy cane geraniums." Gladys shifted her gaze from the flowers to the baby. A soft smile lifted her lips. "Hello, Caleb. Aren't you the handsome boy? I love your blue hat."

Marigold beamed as if Gladys had given *her* the compliment. "I hope you're on your way to Ami's, because this little guy and I are ready to party with you."

"Wouldn't miss it. I have my gift right here." Gladys patted the colorful bag looped over her shoulder.

"You didn't need to bring another gift," Marigold protested. "The quilt you gave Caleb when we brought him home is amazing and more than enough."

"A child can't have too many presents or too much love." Gladys lightly stroked the baby's back.

"I told Cade this morning that I can't believe we started June childless, and we'll end the month with a baby in our arms and one on the way." Despite knowing this was real life and not a big-screen musical, Marigold had to fight the urge to burst into song and dance down the sidewalk.

"This is only the start of the big changes coming your way." Gladys's comment rang like a prophecy.

Marigold frowned. She'd never been a fan of cryptic comments, and she didn't appreciate vague hints. Especially from a woman many believed could see into the future.

"That's the second time you've said something like that to me. You need to spell out exactly what you mean, Gladys. You're scaring me. Are you referring to us having two babies or something else?"

Gladys's pale blue eyes glittered. "Two babies. Yes. That's exactly what I'm talking about."

Marigold expelled the breath she hadn't realized she was holding.

Gladys smiled and, with an ease born of decades of experience, changed the subject. "Your husband was wise to meet with Beck and review the adoption documents ahead of time."

"I didn't realize that's what their meeting was about until we were presented with the legal forms in the hospital. Cade told me the wording had already been reviewed by Beck." Marigold recalled that day at Muddy Boots when she'd seen Cade and Beck emerge from the back. Those worries now seemed a lifetime ago.

"Listen to the music." Gladys cocked her head as Ami and Beck's home came into view. "And if I'm not mistaken, that's Ruby laughing like a hyena."

Sounds of community. People coming together. All ages. Laughing. Talking. Celebrating.

Marigold paused outside the black wrought-iron gate. Inside the fence were her people, her village.

Like a video playing in slow motion, she saw her years at the Chicago salon where she'd built her reputation as a premier hairstylist. Images of her return to Good Hope and falling in love with Cade had a smile lifting her lips.

More than her family had embraced her return. The community had rallied and supported her when she'd opened her own salon.

Now, change had come again, this time in the form of the eight-pound, eleven-ounce baby boy sleeping against her chest. And in the form of a tiny embryo—now as big as a raspberry—growing inside her.

Her business would soon expand as she and Charlotte forged a partnership for Marigold's Golden Door Salon and Day Spa, an arrangement that would leave Marigold with more time for family and friends.

"Sometimes I want to pinch myself. This is like one big, amazing dream." Marigold expelled a happy sigh. "I've been blessed beyond what I could have imagined."

"You and Cade are going to fill that big home of yours with children." Gladys shot her a wink. "I firmly believe you're up to the challenge."

"I appreciate your confidence. I'll certainly do my best."

"Marigold."

She turned toward the sound of her name. Her three sisters hurried across the lawn toward her. As she waved at them, out of the corner of her eye she saw her husband's cruiser pull to the curb.

When he stepped out and smiled, a warm feeling of thankfulness enveloped Marigold, and she knew she was right where she was meant to be.

Building a life with the man she loved.

Surrounded by family she adored.

Embraced by friends who understood and accepted her.

Forging a business path that gave her pride and satisfaction.

Marigold gazed down at the baby who snuggled against her, his tiny rosebud of a mouth moving in sleep.

All her dreams, down to the last one, were coming true in Good Hope.

Cade slid an arm around her shoulders. He smiled. "Who's ready to party?"

~

This resolution has been a long time coming...and it makes it even sweeter. Cade and Marigold started trying to have a baby shortly after they got married. But while her sisters seemed to have no trouble filling their nurseries, a baby didn't seem to be in their future.

Thank you for coming along with Cade and Marigold on this journey. One that is only beginning.

If you're new to the Good Hope series, you've seen that you can enjoy one book without having read all the others before it... but I believe you'll love reading Cade and Marigold's book, BE MINE IN GOOD HOPE, to see how it all began.

Buy BE MINE IN GOOD HOPE now and start reading immediately (or keep reading for a sneak peek)

Chapter One

"Marigold."

Her sister's joyful squeal split the air a second before Marigold Bloom found herself enfolded in Prim's arms. She let herself be hugged tight. Only when tears stung the backs of her eyes did she recognize the danger and pull back.

"You look fabulous." Prim's hazel eyes, so like their father's, shone with undisguised delight.

"You're the one who looks fabulous." Marigold held her sister at arms' length. "Simply stunning."

Prim's shimmery green silk flattered her strawberry blonde curls and porcelain complexion. If Marigold had been around prior to the party, she'd have twisted Prim's hair up instead of letting it fall to her shoulders. The up-do would have added a touch of elegance, especially with some pearls woven through the silky strands.

"Does Ami know you're here?" Even as she asked the question, Prim surveyed the crowd as if searching for their eldest sister.

"Happy New Year, Marigold." Max Brody, Prim's husband of

four months, stepped forward and lightly brushed a welcoming kiss across her cheek.

"Same to you, Max." Marigold liked her new brother-in-law, but the growing concern in his blue eyes said he saw too much. She squeezed her sister's arm. "I'll catch up with you in a bit. Right now I'm off in search of a big glass of champagne and our wonderful hostess."

As Marigold wove her way through the crowd, she was reminded of another party. A party where, like tonight, champagne flowed freely and music and conversation filled the air. She may have started that particular evening alone, but she'd ended it in the arms of a handsome gray-eyed stranger.

How many times, Marigold wondered, had she revisited that particular interlude over the past eighteen months? *Too many times to count.*

Her life might be unraveling quicker than a row of dropped stitches, but memories of that one perfect night still had the power to buoy her spirits.

Marigold's lips curved as a thought struck her. When she'd left Chicago this afternoon, she wondered how she was going to distract a brain that kept reliving the events of the past forty-eight hours ad nauseam. She now had a plan. Instead of ruminating about the mess that was now her life, she'd ruminate on her one-and-only one-night stand.

Her mood had swung from *despairing* to *almost cheerful* when she was stopped by David and Whitney Chapin. She'd once been friends with David's younger sister but hadn't known him all that well. And Whitney? Well, despite the couple's ten-year marriage, Marigold could count on one hand the number of times she'd seen the woman.

"Beck didn't mention you were back in town." David smiled a warm welcome. He was a handsome man with dark hair and eyes that reminded her of gray fog.

"It's a surprise visit." Marigold widened her smile to include his wife, who managed to look both bored and elegant in a shimmery bronze dress that showed off her tanned and toned body to perfection.

The woman reminded Marigold of many of the clients she'd had in Chicago. Whitney's hair, a rich mahogany color with burgundy highlights, was shorter than Marigold remembered from the last time their paths had crossed. The textured razor cut parted on the side flattered her angular face and was clearly the work of an expert.

"It's great you could come for the party." David glanced around, his gaze lingering for a second on the pretty tables laden with appetizers and desserts. "Beck and Ami did it up right and they got a great turn-out. I told Whitney I was looking forward to seeing everyone."

"And I told you that all these same people will be at the Valentine dance." Whitney waved a hand adorned with a glittery diamond the size of Texas. "There was no need for us to celebrate New Year's in Good Hope."

Though his pleasant expression never wavered, a muscle in David's jaw jumped before his gaze shifted from his wife back to Marigold.

"I wouldn't have seen you if I hadn't come." David smiled, obviously assuming this was a brief visit and she'd be long gone before next month's festivities.

Dear God, Marigold hoped that was the case. On top of everything else going wrong, the last thing she'd want was to be the third wheel with her sisters and their husbands at the big V-Day dance.

There was not a single doubt in Marigold's mind that a question--or two--about her plans was poised on David's lips. Searching for a way to graciously exit the conversation, she murmured a silent prayer of thanks when she spotted Hadley Newhouse.

"Hadley." Marigold raised her voice to be heard above the din. When the pretty blonde turned, she motioned her over.

Hadley gave Marigold a hug when she reached her, then cast a curious glance in David and Whitney's direction.

"Hi, David." Hadley offered him a polite smile then extended her hand to Whitney. "I don't believe we've met. I'm Hadley Newhouse. I work at Bloom's Bake Shop. Your husband and daughter stop in occasionally. Brynn is adorable."

Whitney's lips lifted in a smile so brief, Marigold knew she and Hadley both would have missed it if they hadn't been looking.

"Have you seen Ami, Hadley?" Marigold broke the awkward silence. "I haven't spoken with her yet."

"I know exactly where she is and she'll definitely want to see you right away." Hadley grabbed the life preserver Marigold tossed her with both hands. "I'll take you to her."

"That'd be fabulous." After saying good-byes to David and Whitney, the two women slipped into the crowd.

"Whitney is a beautiful woman." Marigold kept her tone low. "Too bad she has the personality of a gnat."

Hadley chuckled. "Rumor is she wanted to spend New Year's in New York and isn't happy about being here."

"The best laid plans…" Marigold murmured, thinking of her own.

"Speaking of plans." Hadley's eyes narrowed. "What are you doing back in Good Hope?"

"Long story." Marigold kept her tone light and refused to meet Hadley's scrutinizing gaze. "One best told over chocolate and wine."

"And, I would suspect, with family." Hadley gave her shoulder a supportive squeeze. "Let's find big sister."

With Hadley's help, Ami soon came into view. Her eldest sister stood next to their father and--Marigold barely suppressed a shudder--Anita Fishback, their father's girlfriend.

Ami's husband stood beside his wife, his hand resting supportively on her shoulder.

Marigold was thankful Ami had Beck to lean on. When their mother died eight years ago, Ami had taken over her role as family nurturer. No one in the family could comfort and soothe as well as the eldest Bloom sister.

While Marigold was in desperate need of some 'mothering,' now wasn't the time. The eldest Bloom sister had a party to host.

"Thanks for the company, Hadley." Marigold flashed a smile. "Now that I know where Ami is, I'm going to grab a glass of champagne and wait for her to finish speaking with Anita."

"Steering clear of the piranha is always a smart move." Hadley went on to regale her with a recent Anita 'antic.'

Marigold found herself listening with only half an ear. Like a hunting dog spotting its prey, her senses now quivered with anticipation. From past experience she knew this was someone who could keep her happily occupied for hours. Someone who wouldn't ask too many questions.

The man had dark hair and a lean, athletic build. Smoky gray eyes glittered when their gazes locked. Best of all, the man who'd once been a stranger, was now headed straight for her.

～

Cade Rallis spotted Marigold the second she strolled into the parlor. He'd been standing with his back to the wall, lazily surveying the room and debating with Jeremy Rakes which teams would make it to the Super Bowl when he saw her. At that moment Cade knew his conversation with Good Hope's Mayor was destined to come to a quick end.

As he and Jeremy continued their spirited discussion, Cade bided his time until Marigold broke free of Hadley.

"Bottom line. The Patriots might make it to the Super Bowl again but they won't win." Cade handed his empty champagne glass to a male server passing by, clapped Jeremy on the shoulder and strode off.

He heard someone call his name but didn't turn. When only several feet separated him and Marigold, Cade slowed his pace. With her tumble of blonde hair and pretty elfin features, Marigold Bloom reminded him of a fairy who might flit away if startled.

Though dressed far more casually than the other party-goers, she still managed to be the most beautiful woman in the room.

"What a nice surprise." He stepped close, let his gaze linger. "I didn't expect to see you here."

"It's my sister's party." Marigold flashed a smile that lifted those luscious ruby lips but didn't quite reach her eyes. "Attending was a last minute decision."

Which meant she'd hit the blizzard currently raging between Chicago and Good Hope. That explained the lines of strain around her eyes. "How were the roads?"

She lifted one shoulder, let it drop in a careless gesture. "I've seen worse."

"That's a long drive even in the best of conditions." Cade wondered if she'd taken time to eat. He recalled the one evening —and night—they'd spent together. At the wedding reception she'd been so focused on having fun she'd forgotten to fuel up. "I bet you skipped dinner."

"Maybe."

The coy smile lifting the tips of her wide mouth told Cade he'd hit the mark. He placed a palm against her back. "Let's scout up some hors d'oeuvres."

She glanced off to the side, her gaze briefly pausing on where her oldest sister stood before returning to him. "What's tasty?"

Cade rocked back on the heels of the shiny black shoes he'd rented, along with the tux, for tonight's party. Black tie was foreign territory. He'd grown up around soldiers, hung out with fellow cops as an adult. Past New Year's Eves were usually welcomed in with bottles of beer and thick cuts of salami and cheese.

"All the appetizers I've tried have been good," he responded when he realized Marigold was waiting for an answer. He smiled ruefully. "I'm not certain what's in some of them. Truth is, I'm not sure I want to know."

Because the sparkle in her eyes was so warm and friendly, he leaned close and confided. "I'm a fish out of water here."

"If you are, it doesn't show. You look as if you were born to wear a tux." She reached up and fingered his lapel. "It's an incredibly sexy look."

As her gaze met his and held, Cade felt the same flare of heat he'd experienced when they'd met at his cousin's wedding. Things at the Detroit Police Department had been tense at the time. He'd been ready to kick back and relax. The time spent with Marigold had been the best part of his trip to Door County.

"If we want pizza," he heard himself say, "we won't find it here."

Marigold laughed softly. The sudden flare of heat in her eyes told him she remembered that they'd been naked the last time they shared a pizza.

"We could slip out." He offered an easy smile. "Grab a slice at the new place down by the pier."

She'd been restless that weekend and he sensed the same edginess now. Cade had no illusions she'd end up in his bed tonight, although that would be nice. Right now, he only hoped for an hour or two alone with her. She was a fascinating woman; one he'd like to get to know better.

"My truck isn't far," he said when she appeared to hesitate. "The pizza will be my treat."

Marigold opened her mouth but before she could speak, her sister Ami appeared and pulled her close.

"I can't believe you're here. When I saw you across the room I thought I was hallucinating. But then Beck said he saw you, too. I nearly knocked over a waiter getting to you." Ami paused to take a breath, looped her arm firmly through her sister's and shot Cade a warning glance. "Marigold is not going anywhere tonight. My baby sister is ringing in the New Year right here."

He lifted his hands in a gesture of surrender. "Simply offering options."

Cade wondered if Ami saw the pain behind Marigold's bright smile. He didn't have a chance to do more than wonder when Beck clapped a hand on his shoulder. "Do you have a moment?"

"Sure. What's up?"

Beckett Cross was a straight-shooter and a savvy business-man. In the six months since Cade had arrived in Good Hope, they'd become friends.

"I'm about to rope you into some volunteering." Beck slanted a glance at his wife. "Fashion Show. Valentine's dance. Or leading a Seedlings troop. Which will it be, Rallis?"

Cade winced. Ever since he'd taken over the role of interim sheriff last summer he'd been approached weekly about various volunteer 'opportunities.' While he wanted to give back to the community that had welcomed him so freely, learning the ins and outs of the department responsible for protecting this town was a full-time job.

But seeing the determined gleam in Beck's eyes told Cade that he wasn't going to be able to play the 'I'm settling into my job' card much longer. Had *fashion show* really been one of the options? Cade took a step back.

"Give him time to digest the options, Beck." Marigold slipped her arm through Cade's. "Right now the sheriff owes me a dance."

"You haven't even told us what you're doing back in Good Hope," Ami protested, concern furrowing her brow.

"Enjoy your guests." In what appeared to be an attempt to mollify her sister, Marigold leaned over and brushed a kiss across Ami's cheeks, then wiped off the lipstick with her thumb. "We can chat later."

Ami's jaw jutted out at a stubborn tilt. "Tell me one thing. Are you in trouble?"

If Cade hadn't been a trained observer and if his gaze hadn't been focused on the woman at his side, he wouldn't have noticed Marigold's barely perceptible hesitation.

"Trouble?" Marigold gave a little laugh and, if possible, smiled even more brightly. She gestured to the crowd with a sweep of one hand. "I'm good. You know me. I'm impulsive. I simply couldn't think of a better place to party in a new year, so here I am."

The tense set to Ami's shoulders eased. Although Cade could tell her sister wasn't completely convinced—smart woman--she appeared willing to give Marigold the benefit of the doubt. For now.

"Well, I'm glad you came." Warmth and love laced through Ami's words. "If Fin were here, I'd have all my sisters with me. I can't imagine a more glorious way to ring in another year."

Though Cade couldn't see anything distressing about Ami's comment, Marigold's fingers tightened around his bicep.

"I like this song," he announced as the music changed to a slow, romantic ballad likely popular when his great-grandfather had been in high school. Cade fixed his gaze on Marigold. "Let's dance."

Relief flickered in her eyes. Her sunny smile never wavered. "Let's."

Marigold turned to her sister and brother-in-law. "Mind if I spend the night?"

The request put to rest any hope Cade still harbored of Marigold ringing in the new year in his bed.

Pleasure tinged with relief rippled across Ami's face. "I wouldn't have it any other way."

"You're always welcome," Beck added. "Stay as long as you like."

"Thank you." Marigold's voice wavered slightly but Cade didn't think Ami or Beck noticed.

Marigold didn't say another word. Instead, with that bright smile still fixed to those pretty red lips, she dragged Cade across the parlor toward the music and dancers in the adjoining room.

Curl up with this heartwarming romance that will keep you turning the page and leave you with a smile on your face. Grab your copy now. BE MINE IN GOOD HOPE

ALSO BY CINDY KIRK

Good Hope Series

The Good Hope series is a must-read for those who love stories that uplift and bring a smile to your face.

Check out the entire Good Hope series here

Hazel Green Series

Readers say "Much like the author's series of Good Hope books, the reader learns about a town, its people, places and stories that enrich the overall experience. It's a journey worth taking."

Check out the entire Hazel Green series here

Holly Pointe Series

Readers say "If you are looking for a festive, romantic read this Christmas, these are the books for you."

Check out the entire Holly Pointe series here

Jackson Hole Series

Heartwarming and uplifting stories set in beautiful Jackson Hole, Wyoming.

Check out the entire Jackson Hole series here

Silver Creek Series

Engaging and heartfelt romances centered around two powerful families whose fortunes were forged in the Colorado silver mines.

Check out the entire Silver Creek series here

Made in the USA
Las Vegas, NV
07 November 2021

33936712R00052